D0710792

YOUNG VIC

The Young Vic Theatre Company presents

More Grimm Tales

Adapted by **Carol Ann Duffy**
Directed by **Tim Supple**
Dramatised by **The Young Vic Company**

faber and faber
LONDON · BOSTON

The Young Vic is supported by

Production sponsored by

THE YOUNG VIC THEATRE

In 1968 Lord Olivier and the National Theatre (then based at the Old Vic) talked of a theatre which would form a centre of work particularly accessible to students and young people. The theatre's programme was to include the classics, new plays and educational work, and would provide an opportunity for young performers, writers and directors to develop their craft.

The Young Vic was established in September 1970 by Frank Dunlop and became the first major theatre producing work for younger audiences. In 1974 the Young Vic became independent of the National and went on to establish an international reputation for its productions, developing a wide-ranging audience of all ages and backgrounds.

In its 27 years the theatre has created an enormous range and style of work, from Beckett to Sophocles and Shakespeare to John Lennon, including the professional world première of *Joseph and the Amazing Technicolor Dreamcoat* (Tim Rice and Andrew Lloyd Webber) and Arthur Miller's *The Last Yankee*. More recent highly successful Young Vic productions include Tim Supple's *The Slab Boys Trilogy*, written by John Byrne; the enormous hit *Grimm Tales*, which toured to Hong Kong, Australia and New Zealand; a stage adaptation of four stories from Kipling's *The Jungle Book*; *Blood Wedding* by Federico Garcìa Lorca in a new version by Ted Hughes; Martin Crimp's version of Molière's *The Misanthrope* and David Mamet's *American Buffalo*, both directed by Lindsay Posner; a translation of Strinberg's *Miss Julie* by Meredith Oakes, directed by Polly Teale, *Beauty and the Beast*, directed by Laurence Boswell, and *King Lear* with Kathryn Hunter in the title role.

Recent collaborations have included a presentation of Tim Supple's RSC production of *The Comedy of Errors*, and a co-production with Shared Experience of *Jane Eyre*, directed by Polly Teale.

The Young Vic continues its commitment to creating adventurous theatre for as wide an audience as possible and particularly the young. As London's only purpose-built theatre-in-the-round and most adaptable thrust stage, the Young Vic offers unique opportunities for intimate ensemble performance and the imaginative use of space, light and sound.

'Both the building and the stage/audience relationship are unique and altogether vital to the theatre scene of the metropolis' TREVOR NUNN

THE YOUNG VIC THEATRE COMPANY
Arts for Everyone: A New National Lottery Funding Scheme

The Young Vic is delighted to announce that it was recently awarded one of the highest grants in the country under the new National Lottery Arts For Everyone Scheme. This award is for a daring project of new creative work and associated audience development which will allow the Young Vic to build upon its growth over the last three years and further establish its position as one of the premier theatre companies in the country.

In detail, this prestigious award enables the Young Vic to implement key artistic and education initiatives including: the development of a permanent company of actors and musicians to create new shows with longer rehearsal periods and higher production values (of which *More Grimm Tales* is the first); the encouragement of young artists on the cutting edge of performance to develop their work through experimentation in the Young Vic's award winning Studio; significant and integrated growth in the Young Vic's existing audience development programme (The Funded Ticket Scheme – main sponsor Allied Domecq) into one of the largest audience access initiatives ever seen, particularly amongst young people; and, finally, the award provides vital resources for a substantial and significant increase in the breadth and width of the Young Vic's acclaimed education work with children, students, teachers and young professionals.

The Arts For Everyone programme is designed to highlight the integral role that a theatre plays in the community. To realise the enormous potential that this award promises, the Young Vic must find companies or individuals who share in a belief of the vital importance of such investment in the community – over the next three years the Young Vic must raise a total of £100,000 in partnership funding to release this remarkable lottery award.

If you would like more information on how you can contribute to, or participate in this unique and exciting time at the Young Vic then please phone 0171 633 0133.

SUPPORT THE YOUNG VIC
Become a Friend

'The Young Vic is a vital resource in London' PETE TOWNSHEND

'The Young Vic is a unique part of our theatre heritage'
DAME JUDI DENCH

'The Young Vic audience offers proof that the theatre is alive
in our time' ARTHUR MILLER

Join our Friends Scheme and your support will immediately help the Young Vic
continue to create outstanding, innovative theatre. Becoming a friend also enables
you to join more fully in the life of the theatre by taking advantage of these
excellent benefits:

Friend £20.00 annual subscription
- **Two half-price preview tickets to all Young Vic Company productions**
- **Regular advance information • Priority booking • Invitations to special
  Friends performances**

Supporting Friend £50.00 annual subscription
- **Six half-price preview tickets to all Young Vic Company productions**
- **Regular advance information • Priority booking • Reserved seating**
- **Invitations to special Friends performances**

Junior Friend £5.00 annual subscription
If you are under 16 years of age, become a Junior Friend for only £5.00 per year
and receive:
- **Your own personal Young Vic card • Regular advance information**
- **Invitations to Junior Friends performances**

To find out more about the advantages of becoming a Young Vic Friend, or to join
the free mailing list, call Philip Spedding, on **0171 633 0133**, or pick up a leaflet in
the foyer.

The work of the Young Vic receives support from:
Anonymous, Allied Domecq, The Baring Foundation, British Steel, Kids Connections,
Time Out Kids Out, Frogmore Estates plc., The John Lewis Partnership, The Newcomen
Collett Foundation, The Persula Foundation, The Peter Minet Trust, The Rayne Foundation,
The Reuter Foundation, Royal & Sunalliance and our many Young Vic Friends.

THE YOUNG VIC STUDIO

"The Young Vic's diverse repertoire from the edge is London's most daring theatre-going experience" TIME OUT

The Young Vic Studio is dedicated to housing and nurturing experiments in writing, music, performance and design. It is an environment in which the encouragement of creativity and collaboration is the vital driving force.

The Young Vic Studio this Winter

2 - 20 December
Strathcona Theatre Company present *Change of Heart*
A wicked demon... a magical mirror shattered into millions of pieces... hearts turned to ice. Into the world of the Snow Queen steps a young person with Down's Syndrome desperately ill and needing transplant surgery leaving behind a hospital ward where an ethical and legal battle rages all around.

22 December - 3 January
Springtime Productions present *Dearest Daddy... Darling Daughter*
A celebration of father-daughter relationships in words and music, featuring Julia and Nadia Sawalha, Janine Buckley and Nadim Sawalha. Dad and three daughters get together for an evening of literary, dramatic and musical reveries on fathers and daughters.

6 - 17 January
Desperate Optimists present *Stalking Realness*
How do we find value and meaning and a sense of our true identity – no matter how fragile or flawed – in the world we have constructed for ourselves? To look for answers, is it better to turn to the banal, the familiar, the mundane, the innocuous, the accidental and the things we just can't control?

To book tickets for all Young Vic Studio performances call
0171 928 6363

The Young Vic Theatre Company presents

More Grimm Tales

Performers *in alphabetical order*

Robert Bowman
Sarah C. Cameron
Thusitha Jayasundera
Linda Kerr Scott
Paul Meston
Dan Milne
Christopher Saul
Andy Williams
Leo Wringer

Musicians

Simon Allen
Percussion, vibraphone, hammer dulcimer, surmandal, mbira
Sylvia Hallett
Vocals, viola, violin, kemençe, rebec, accordion, hurdy-gurdy, Mexican harp
Adrian Lee
Mandola, 'ud, siter, keyboards, percussion

Adapted by **Carol Ann Duffy**
Dramatised by **The Young Vic Company**
Directed by **Tim Supple**
Designed by **Melly Still**
Composer & Musical Director **Adrian Lee**
Lighting designed by **Paule Constable**
Sound designed by **Paul Bull**
Associate Director (voice, text & movement) **Barbara Houseman**
Assistant Director **Craig Higginson**
Assistant Designer **Natalie Gibbs**
Costume Supervisor **Anna Watkins**
Puppet instruction by **Ronnie Le Drew**

PRODUCTION ACKNOWLEDGMENTS
The Young Vic gratefully acknowledges the assistance of **Persil**, **Comfort** and **Persil Finesse**, courtesy of **Lever Brothers Ltd.**, in providing Wardrobe care.
Puppets made by the **Little Angel Theatre** (Chief Carver **Jan Zalud**).
Props made by **Alex Tuppen**.
Contribution to musical arrangements by **Simon Allen** and **Sylvia Hallet**.
Lighting equipment supplied by **Sparks Theatrical Hire**, **White Light (Electrics) Ltd.**, and **Lighting Technology**.

This production is supported in part by The German Embassy

The performance will last approximately 2 hours with one interval.
First performed at the Young Vic on **24 November, 1997**.

Cast in order of appearance

Little Red-Cap
Red-Cap **Sarah C. Cameron**
Mother/Grandmother **Linda Kerr Scott**
Wolf **Andy Williams**
Hunter **Leo Wringer**

Clever Hans
Clever Hans **Dan Milne**
Mother **Christopher Saul**
Gretel **Thusitha Jayasundera**

The Hare and the Hedgehog
Narrator **Paul Meston**
Hedgehog **Robert Bowman**
Hare **Dan Milne**
Hedgehog's Wife **Sarah C. Cameron**

Snow White
Narrator/Mirror
Christopher Saul
Mother/Queen **Leo Wringer**
Snow White **Thusitha Jayasundera**
Hunter **Robert Bowman**
Disguised Queen
Linda Kerr Scott
Prince **Dan Milne**

The Musicians of Bremen
Donkey **Andy Williams**
Dog **Paul Meston**
Cat **Leo Wringer**
Cock **Dan Milne**

Rumpelstiltskin
Miller **Christopher Saul**
Miller's Daughter **Sarah C. Cameron**
King/Messenger **Robert Bowman**
Rumpelstiltskin **Linda Kerr Scott**

Brother Scamp
Brother Scamp **Paul Meston**
St Peter **Christopher Saul**

All other parts played by the
Company.

At various times during the perfor-
mance, some or all of the following
stories may also be told:
Fair Katrinelje
The Fox and the Geese
The Golden Key
Knoist and His Three Sons
The Sweet Porridge
Travelling
Two Households
The Ungrateful Son
The Wise Servant

BIOGRAPHIES

SIMON ALLEN *Musician*
Simon Allen is a percussionist and composer whose abilities combine a classical training with the experienced study of other music cultures. Working mainly in contemporary music, dance and theatre, he records regularly for Radio 3 both as a soloist and with groups such as *The Dangerous Kitchen* and *George W.Welch*. Compositions include works for *Impressions* (Radio 3), KPM Film and Television Music Library, Mark Baldwin Dance Company and the 1991 Japan Festival. Work as a musician in theatre includes *The Comedy of Errors* (RSC/Young Vic). As an instrument maker he collaborated with Egyptian sculptor Gamal Abdel Nasser for exhibitions and performances at the Delfina Studio Gallery (London 1995) and Espace Karim Frances (Cairo 1996). He is active in music education from Primary level to postgraduate, including The Philharmonic Orchestra, Guildhall School of Music and Drama, London Contemporary Dance Trust, and is a co-founder of South London Arts Project.

ROBERT BOWMAN *Performer*
Trained: The School of the Science of Acting & The Guildhall School of Music & Drama. Theatre Includes work at The Focus Theatre, The Abbey Theatre, Leeds Playhouse, York Theatre Royal, West Yorkshire Playhouse, Hackney Empire, The Gate Theatre, The Royal National Theatre, The Royal Shakespeare Company, and the Young Vic. Radio includes *The Woods*, *Pioneers in Inglostadt*. Television includes *The Wastehouse Farm Murders*, *Of Pure Blood*.

PAUL BULL *Sound Designer*
Work includes national and international tours with The Kosh and Rambert Dance Company, and a production of Miranda Richardson's one woman show *Orlando* at the 1996 Edinburgh Festival. He has designed sound for shows in venues ranging from pub theatres to the West End, as well as many touring companies. Paul spent most of the 1980s as Chief Sound Technician for the Leicester Haymarket Theatre.

SARAH C. CAMERON *Performer*
Trained: Ecole Jacques Lecoq, Paris. Theatre includes *The Comedy of Errors* (RSC/Young Vic), *The Jungle Book* (Young Vic), *Grimm Tales* (Young Vic & tour to Hong Kong, Australia & New Zealand), *A Call in the Night* (West Yorkshire

Playhouse), *Alicesongs* (Manchester Library Theatre), *Beulah Land* (ICA), *Marjorie Stuart and the Apocalypse* (one woman show – Chisendale Dance Space), *Gormenghast* (David Glass Ensemble, BAC, Lyric Hammersmith & UK tour), *Lipstick Tango* (Croydon Warehouse). Television includes *Knowing Me Knowing You*, *Fist of Fun*.

PAULE CONSTABLE *Lighting Designer*
Previously at the Young Vic: *Omma - Oedipus and the Luck of Thebes*, *The Slab Boys Trilogy*, *The Jungle Book*. Other theatre includes *The Street of Crocodiles*, *The Three Lives of Lucy Cabrol*, *Out of a House Walked a Man*, *The Caucasian Chalk Circle* (all Theatre de Complicite), *Spring Awakening*, *The Mysteries*, *Beckett Shorts* (all RSC), *The Wier* (Royal Court), *Macbeth* (Bristol Old Vic), and *Poor Superman* (Manchester Royal Exchange). Operas include *Don Giovanni* (Welsh National Opera), *Innes de Castro* (Scottish Opera), *The Magic Flute* (Opera North), *Life With an Idiot* (ENO).

CAROL ANN DUFFY *Adaptation*
Carol Ann Duffy is one of Britain's most important contemporary poets and was awarded an OBE for services to poetry in 1995. Her books include *Standing Female Nude* (1985), *Selling Manhattan* (1987), *The Other Country* (1990) and *Mean Time* (1993). Critically acclaimed, her poetry has won an extraordinary number of awards, including The Scottish Arts Council Book Award of Merit (1985), The Somerset Maugham Award (1988), The Dylan Thomas Award (1989), The Cholmondeley Award (1992), The Forward Poetry Prize (1993) and The Whitbread Poetry Award (1993). Her work for theatre includes two plays which have been staged at the Liverpool Playhouse, one for the Not the RSC Festival at the Almeida Theatre, and the adaptation of Grimm Tales at the Young Vic, which toured to Hong Kong, Australia and New Zealand.

NATALIE GIBBS *Assistant Designer*
Trained at Motley. Theatre includes *Linger* (Royal Court at The Clink Vaults), *Mad for Love* (Riverside Studios), *Frankie* and *Mia* (both Grace Theatre), *Subject to Change* (ENO Contemporary Opera Studios), *Twelfth Night* (The Lost Theatre). Work as design assistant includes *The Country Wife* (Theatre Royal, Plymouth), *Il Turco in Italia* (Broomhill), *HRH* (Birmingham Rep), *The Impor-*

tance of Being Earnest (Tel Aviv), *Women Laughing* (Watford Palace Theatre), *Mask of Orpheus* (Royal Festival Hall), *Misper* (Glyndebourne). Work as costume designer includes a tour for The Mark Baldwin Dance Company (Edinburgh, The Place Theatre & The Royal Festival Hall). Future projects include *Anna Karenina* at the Theatre Royal, Plymouth.

SYLVIA HALLETT *Musician*
Sylvia Hallett studied music at Dartington, and then spent two years in Paris studying composition with Max Deutsch. She now works both as a composer and as an improviser, and has had pieces performed in Britain and Europe. As an improviser, she has played in many international festivals since the late 1970s. This has included work with Lol Coxhill, Maggie Nicols and Phil Minton. She is currently in three groups: *British Summer Time Ends*, *Arc*, and *Accordions Go Crazy*. Sylvia Hallett is also involved in projects with various theatre companies. She frequently collaborates with the choreographers/dancers Miranda Tufnell and Emilyn Claid, and the live art puppeteers, *DooCot*. She performed in the world tour of the Young Vic's production of *Grimm Tales* and was a musician for *The Comedy of Errors* (RSC/Young Vic). Recordings: Two solo CDs on the MASH label, and numerous recordings with the above mentioned groups.

CRAIG HIGGINSON *Assistant Director*
Craig Higginson was born in Zimbabwe, and grew up and was educated in South Africa. Work in South Africa includes Assistant Director to Barney Simon at the Market Theatre, Johannesburg. This work includes Berkoff's *East*, *The Suit* and assisting with *Jozi Jozi* (both LIFT '95). He came to London in 1996 and worked as a freelance writer. Work includes reviews for Time Out and writing for Out Of Lift '96, as well as for other theatre and music festivals. He has published poetry in South Africa, England, Ireland and America. His first novel, entitled *Embodied Laughter*, will be published early in 1998.

BARBARA HOUSEMAN *Associate Director (voice, text & movement)*
Barbara Houseman trained as a voice teacher at the Central School of Speech and Drama and as a director at the Bristol Old Vic Theatre School. She has worked professionally as a director as well as

teaching in various London drama schools. Between 1991 and 1997 she was a member of the Voice Department at the Royal Shakespeare Company, working in Stratford, at the Barbican and on tour. She is a qualified Healing-Shiatsu practitioner and has been studying body work and practising Mindfulness Meditation for the past eleven years.

THUSITHA JAYASUNDERA *Performer*
Trained: RADA. Theatre includes *Peer Gynt*, *Coriolanus*, *Pentecost*, *Cain*, *The Comedy of Errors* (all RSC). Television includes *Firm Friends*, *The All New Alexei Sayle Show*.

LINDA KERR SCOTT *Performer*
Trained: Ecole Jacques Lecoq, Paris. Theatre includes *Le Grande Voyage* (La Comedie de Caen) *Troilus and Cressida*, *King Lear*, *The Pretenders* (all RSC), *Grimm Tales*, *Sisters* (both Young Vic), *La Traversee du Desert* (Theatre National Chaillot), *No Son of Mine* (Co.Philippe Gaulier), *Please, Please, Please* and *Ave Maria* (both Theatre De Complicite), *Faust 1&2* (Lyric Hammersmith), *Too Clever By Half* (The Old Vic), *Ghetto* (Royal National Theatre), *Giro de Vita* (Hebbel Theatre, Berlin). Television includes *Burning Ambition*, *Peter and the Wolf*.

ADRIAN LEE *Composer/Musical Director*
Composer and multi-instrumentalist, Adrian Lee has collaborated with Tim Supple on several productions for the Royal National Theatre, the Young Vic, and on *The Knight with the Lion*, commissioned by the South Bank Gamelan Players (QEH, 1995). He is Artistic Director of the gamelan orchestra **Srawana** and a member of the Anglo-Egyptian music ensemble, **Maqaam**. Theatre includes *The Comedy of Errors* (RSC), *The Little Clay Cart*, *A Midsummer Night's Dream*, *Gilgamesh*, *Anoman Obong* (all RNT), *Grimm Tales*, *The Jungle Book*, *Blood Wedding* (all Young Vic), *Dreams of Inanna*, *Shakti*, *Itan-Kahani* (all Pan Project).

PAUL MESTON *Performer*
Trained: LAMDA. Theatre includes *Gilgamesh*, *Macbeth*, *A Midsummer Night's Dream*, *Jo-Jo the Melon Donkey*, *Dragon*, *Le Bourgeois Gentil Homme* (all Royal National Theatre), *Grimm Tales*, *Omma*, *Oedipus & The Luck of Thebes* (all Young Vic), *The Body Politic* (Cockpit Theatre), *Dead*

Funny (Lee Dean Tour), *The Tempest* (Manchester Royal Exchange), *Julius Caesar* (Compass Theatre Co.), *Royal Baccarat Scandal* (Haymarket Theatre), *The Millionairess* (Greenwich Theatre), Television includes *The Bill, Cristabel, Kavanagh QC, Park Life*. Films include *Simoom: A Passion in the Desert, Panther Tango Duck*. Radio includes *Surfers Paradise*.

DAN MILNE *Performer*
Trained: Drama Studio. Theatre includes *The Comedy of Errors* (RSC/Young Vic), Rep - *A Clockwork Orange* (Newcastle), *The Taming of the Shrew* (Worcester), *Master Harold and the Boys* (Milford Haven), *Quasimodo* (Liverpool Everyman), *A Family Affair* (Cheltenham), *Fiddler On the Roof* (Coventry), *The Pied Piper* (Birmingham), *The Island of Dr. Moreau* (York). Theatre in London includes *He Who Saw Everything* (Royal National Theatre), *Celestial Fix* (RNT Studio), *(Small) Objects of Desire* (Soho Theatre Company), *Grimm Tales* (Young Vic & tour to Hong Kong, Australia and New Zealand), *The Jungle Book* (Young Vic). Television includes *It Ain't Cricket, Saturday Night Armistice, Fist of Fun, Murder Most Horrid*.

CHRISTOPHER SAUL *Performer*
Trained: Rose Bruford College. Theatre includes *The Thebans, Columbus: The Discovery of Japan, Breaking the Silence, Hamlet, The Merry Wives of Windsor, Man is Man, Henry IV Part 2, Henry V* (all RSC), *The Comedy of Errors* (RSC/Young Vic), *Want* (RSC Fringe 1991-1992), *The Sea, She Stoops to Conquer, Cabaret, Romeo and Juliet, Benefactors, A Month in the Country, Betrayal, The Rivals, Twelfth Night, Julius Caesar, Just Between Ourselves, Every Good Boy Deserves Favour, The Real Thing, The Winter's Tale, Fiddler on the Roof* (Her Majesty's), *A Variety of Death Defying Acts* (Orange Tree, Richmond), S*tart Right, The Ancient Mariner* (Young Vic). Tours abroad include *Romeo and Juliet* (ESC tour to Germany, Denmark, Japan), *The Comedy of Errors* (ESC tour to USSR, Israel). Television includes *Sharman, London's Burning, The Bill, Grange Hill, Castles, 99 to 1, Between the Lines, Rides, The Chief, Waterfront Beat, Chain, One Foot in the Grave, Small Zones, Poirot, Casualty, Watching, Brookside, Dr. Who, Pericles, Game, Set and Match, Triangle*. Films include *Wilt, Mountbatten:The Last Viceroy*.

MELLY STILL *Designer*
Melly Still is a painter and choreographer. Previous designs for the Young Vic include *Grimm Tales, The Jungle Book*, and *Blood Wedding*.

TIM SUPPLE *Director*
Artistic Director of the Young Vic since 1993. At York Theatre Royal, directed work by Brecht, Kroetz, Shakespeare, Miller and Willy Russell; also Associate Director of Youth Theatre Yorkshire. As Associate Director at the Leicester Haymarket Theatre directed *Oh, What A Lovely War!* and was responsible for all community work. Co-adapted and directed *Billy Budd* (The Crucible, Sheffield). Directed John Sessions' one man show *Travelling Tales, Coriolanus* (Renaissance Theatre Company), *Tamburlaine* (Marlowe Society, Cambridge). At RNT directed his own adaptation of *Gilgamesh*. Also directed *Whale, Accidental Death of an Anarchist* (tour) - new adaptation co-written with Alan Cumming, *Billy Liar* (tour). For the RSC: *Spring Awakening, The Comedy of Errors* (UK and international tour). For the Young Vic, work includes *Omma, The Slab Boys Trilogy, Grimm Tales, The Jungle Book, Blood Wedding*.

ANDY WILLIAMS *Performer*
Trained: Bretton Hall & The Desmond Jones School of Mime. Theatre includes *The Comedy of Errors* (RSC/Young Vic), *The Jungle Book* (Young Vic). Tours include *Bouncers* (Hull Truck Tour including Edinburgh Festival and Riverside Studios London), *The Magic Island* (TAG), *Taking Toys From the Boys, Custer's Last Stand, State of the Nation* (Yorkshire Theatre Company), *Vampire* (The Secret Agents). He has also toured as a stand-up comedian. Opera includes *The Mask of Orpheus* (Royal Festival Hall). Television includes *The Series From Hell*. Films include *Hypnodreamdruff*. Writing includes three plays: *Custer's Last Stand, Stab Zombie, Gangshow*.

LEO WRINGER *Performer*
Theatre includes Solinus/Dr.Pinch in *The Comedy of Errors* (RSC/Young Vic), Poseidon in *Women of Troy* (RNT), *Medea* and *Rosmersholm* (Young Vic), title role in *Othello* (Watermill Theatre, Newbury and tour to Osaka and Globe Theatre, Tokyo), Camillo in *The Winter's Tale* (Theatre de Complicite), Mirabell in *The Way of the World* (Theatre Royal, York), Casca in *Julius Caesar* (Royal Exchange, Manchester), title role in

Woyzeck (Bristol Old Vic). Other Shakespearean roles include Autolycus, Puck, Banquo, Launcelot Gobbo and The Porter. New plays include Peter Whelan's *Divine Right* (Birmingham Rep.), Biyi Bandele's *Two Horsemen* (Bush Theatre - 1994 Time Out Actor Award), Howard Korder's *Search and Destroy* (Royal Court), Botho Strauss' *Seven Doors*, Mario Vargos Llosa's *The Madman of the Balconies* (both Gate Theatre, Notting Hill), Bernard Marie-Koltes' *Struggle of the Dogs and the Black* (Traverse Theatre, Edinburgh). Opera includes *Die Entführung Aus Dem Serail* (Garsington Manor). Films include *The Changeling*, *The Kitchen Toto* (winner of the 1986 Tokyo Prize).

THE YOUNG VIC COMPANY

YOUNG VIC COMPANY

66 The Cut, South Bank, London SE1 8LZ

A company limited by guarantee, registered in England No.1188209

VAT Registration No. 236 673348. Charity Registration No. 268876

Box Office **0171 928 6363**

Administration **0171 633 0133**

Press Office **0171 620 0568**

Fax **0171 928 1585**

YOUNG VIC
THEATRE

THE RSC/YOUNG VIC SEASON

RSC
ROYAL
SHAKESPEARE
COMPANY
Sponsored by
ALLIED
DOMECQ

FROM 11 FEBRUARY 1998

HENRY VIII

BY WILLIAM SHAKESPEARE

"splendid...performances fit for a King"
DAILY MAIL

Paul Jesson as Henry VIII

FROM 26 FEBRUARY 1998

CAMINO REAL

BY TENNESSEE WILLIAMS

sponsored by Maker's Mark

*"beautiful revival...
spectacularly good production...
Camino Real emerges as
Tennessee Williams' great
'lost' play"* GUARDIAN

Peter Egan as Casonova

FROM 25 MARCH 1998

UNCLE VANYA

BY ANTON CHEKHOV
ENGLISH TRANSLATION BY DAVID LAN

an RSC/Young Vic co-production

Katie Mitchell's new production of Chekhov's
masterpiece has an outstanding cast including
Stephen Dillane, Anastasia Hille and Linus Roache.

Stephen Dillane as Vanya

BOX OFFICE **0171 928 6363**

**TICKETS FOR THE SEASON GO ON
SALE AT THE END OF DECEMBER**

THE
ARTS
COUNCIL
OF ENGLAND

More Grimm Tales

First published in 1997
by Faber and Faber Limited
3 Queen Square London WC1N 3AU

Typeset by Country Setting, Woodchurch, Kent TN26 3TB
Printed in England by Mackays of Chatham plc, Chatham, Kent

A CIP record for this book
is available from the British Library

ISBN 0-571-19443-5

2 4 6 8 10 9 7 5 3 1

Contents

The Brothers Grimm

Jacob and Wilhelm Grimm (1785–1863 and 1786–1859) were born into a fairly prosperous middle-class family. But the early death of their father, who had risen to become a district magistrate, led to severe financial difficulties and meant that Jacob had to assume the role as head of the house at the age of nine. Through their Aunt, who was a lady-in-waiting to the Princess of Hessia-Kassel, Jacob and Wilhelm gained places at the prestigious local Lyceum, where their financial status and their social position made it imperative that they should succeed. This enabled them to obtain special dispensations to study Law at the University of Marburg, where the brothers caught the attention of Friedrich Carl von Savigny, whose historical perspective on Law would kindle the brothers' interest in German folklore.

Jacob and Wilhelm grew up during the middle period of what is roughly referred to as European Romanticism. Headed in Germany by philosophers like Herder and writers like Heine and the young Goethe, the movement brought a new interest in Germany's past, which was declared a living thing with its own national character. The simplicity of the folk traditions, which had been ignored by Enlightenment thinkers, suddenly acquired a new value. Herder and his followers sought the *Volkseele* or 'folk-psyche' in German and European literature, and they returned to folksongs, ballads and the half-buried masterpieces of German medieval literature. They also emphasised the revival of the folktale, pointing to regional variations and calling for new collections to be made.

With their passionate historicism and their devoted and reverent search for origins of all kinds, the brothers were to become not only the virtual inventors of systematic folklorism, but the pioneers of medievalist scholarship and historical philology. They worked as librarians in Kassel for most of their lives (they had worked as professors at Gottingen but were dismissed from their posts by the new king of Hanover for their liberal political views), which enabled them to continue their studies and write; and, in spite of ongoing financial difficulties, they published in the region of forty books – including studies on German Law, Language, Mythology and Legends; a four volume German Grammar and a massive German Dictionary, of which they compiled only four volumes in their lifetime but which took other scholars until 1961 to complete.

But their most famous collection was their *Kinder- und Hausmarchen* (or 'Children's and Household Tales'). Jacob and Wilhelm had no delusions about the Germanic origins of these tales. They had read previous collections of many of the tales (in particular, Perrault's strongly literary collection, which appeared in Paris in 1797), but their interests lay in the *German* variants of what they knew to be ancient, widely dispersed material (origins for the tales can be found throughout medieval Europe and Asia, and many of them can be traced as far back as Ancient Greece, Egypt and even China). They relied on a variety of sources from Germany, Austria, Bohemia and Switzerland, and interviewed anyone from friends and neighbours to peasants and members of the aristocracy. In 1825 Wilhelm actually married a woman called Dorothea Wild who, along with her sisters and their elderly house-keeper, had provided them with versions of some of their best-known tales. The first volume was published in 1812, and the response was so encouraging that new material flooded in from across the country, and a second volume followed in 1815. The brothers attempted to transcribe the stories as exactly as possible – with bits of nonsense, dialect, rhymes and old sayings included wherever possible. The initial aim was to be 'wholly scholarly', to compile 'materials for the history of German literature', and any aesthetic or entertainment value that they might have had would be merely incidental; but in time the brothers adjusted this, and sometimes edited out material that seemed to them unseemly or tedious.

By Wilhelm's death, seven editions of the tales had been published. Jacob, who had always been the more introverted of the two and who had remained a bachelor throughout his life, was busy on an eighth edition when he died. By the end of the nineteenth century, the tales had been translated widely and were known across Europe. Today they are the most popular and famous collection of folktales in the world.

Craig Higginson

Staging the Tales

The stories from the collection made by the Grimm brothers make extraordinary theatre. We discovered this by accident in 1994 when we presented a selection of famous and less well known tales at the Young Vic. It was clear that a story such as 'Hansel and Gretel' retained the power to hold the collective attention of large audiences of people of all ages: from under five to over ninety. Our collection, called *Grimm Tales*, enjoyed some success, and quite naturally there arose the idea to return to the 201 Grimms' Tales and make a new selection for a new show.

Our aim is simple: to find a dramatic form that retains the natural, wise and beautifully crafted character of the original stories. We have added and changed nothing. All we *have* done is to adapt the original voices of the stories to the modern ear and split their telling between narrator, character, musician and chorus.

It would be natural to ask why we have not adapted and modernised more. After all, these stories grew through the adaptions of many cultures over many countries. To us, however, the Grimms' collection represents a remarkable meeting between the mysterious, eclectic process of folk art and the skills and intentions of two late eighteenth century German Christian writers. In their own way they are as specific and finely poised as any classic work; and, as with the work of Sophocles or Shakespeare, the imagination of each individual will modernise the stories as much as they need. We seek only to tell them with as much clarity and insight as we are capable of. The theatre is a great place to do this: how else today could you get

500 people together in one room to hear and watch a simple story?

Tim Supple

Note on the Dramatization

Wherever possible, we have left the stage directions to speak for themselves through the dialogue or narration of each story. Stage directions have only been included where the narrative has been replaced by action on stage. Also, the stage directions do not describe any of our solutions to the staging of the stories, although anyone who is doing a production and who is interested in how we staged certain difficult moments (like the transformation of the straw into gold in 'Rumpelstiltskin' or the eating of the grandmother and Little Red-Cap by the wolf) is welcome to contact Tim Supple or Adrian Lee at the Young Vic.

Often we have used certain formal devices in the layout of the text, such as a new paragraph for a change in episode or a full stop breaking a sentence in half to indicate the passing of time.

Tim Supple, Craig Higginson

More Grimm Tales

Dramatized by Tim Supple
and
The Young Vic Company

Little Red-Cap

Red-Cap There was once a delicious little girl who was loved by everyone who saw her.

Grandmother But most of all by her grandmother, who was always wondering what treat to give the sweet child next.

Red-Cap Once she sent her a little red cap which suited her so well that she wouldn't wear anything else and she was known from then on as Little Red-Cap.

Mother One day her mother said, 'Little Red-Cap, here are some cakes and a bottle of best wine. Take them to Grandmother. She's been poorly and is still a bit weak and these will do her good. Now, hurry up before it gets too hot. And mind how you go, like a good little girl. And don't go wandering off the path or you'll fall over and break the wine-bottle and then there will be none left for Grandmother. And when you go into her room, make sure you say "Good Morning" nicely, instead of peeping into every corner first!'

Red-Cap 'Don't worry, I'll do everything just as you say.'
  Her grandmother lived out in the wood, a half-an-hour's walk from the village, and as soon as Little Red-Cap stepped into the wood . . .

Wolf A wolf saw her.

Red-Cap Because she didn't know what a wicked animal it was, she wasn't afraid of it.

Wolf 'Good Morning, Little Red-Cap.'

Red-Cap 'Thank you, Wolf.'

Wolf 'And where might you be going so early?'

Red-Cap 'To my grandmother's house.'

Wolf 'And what's that you're carrying under your apron?'

Red-Cap 'Cakes and wine. We were baking yesterday – and my poor grandmother has been ill, so these will strengthen her.'

Wolf 'Where does Grandmother live, Little Red-Cap?'

Red-Cap 'She lives a quarter-of-an-hour's walk from here, under the three big oak trees. Her house has hazel hedges near it. I'm sure you know it.'

Wolf 'How young and sweet and tender she is. I could eat her. She'll make a plumper mouthful for my jaws than the old woman. If I am wily, though, I can have the pair of them!'

The Wolf walks beside Red-Cap for a while.

Wolf 'Look, Little Red-Cap. Open your eyes and see! There are beautiful flowers all around us. And there's wonderful birdsong that you don't even listen to. You just plod straight ahead as though you were going to school – and yet the woods are such fun!'

Red-Cap So Little Red-Cap looked around her; and when she saw the sunbeams seeming to wink at her among the trees, and when she saw the tempting flowers leading away from the straight path, she thought, 'Grandmother will be very pleased if I pick her a bunch of lovely fresh flowers. And it's still early, so I've got plenty of time.' So she ran from the path, among the trees, picking her flowers, and she kept seeing prettier and prettier flowers which led her deeper and deeper into the wood.

4

Wolf But the wolf ran fast and straight to the grand-mother's house . . . And knocked at the door.

Grandmother 'Who's there?'

Wolf 'Only Little Red-Cap bringing you cake and wine. Open the door.'

Grandmother 'Lift the latch. I'm too feeble to get up.'

Wolf So the wolf lifted the latch and the door flew open and without even a word it leapt on the old woman's bed and gobbled her up. Then it pulled her clothes and her night-cap over its wolfy fur, crawled into her bed and closed the curtains.

Red-Cap All this time, Little Red-Cap had been trotting about among the flowers and when she'd picked as many as her arms could hold, she remembered her grand-mother and hurried off to her house. She was surprised to see that the door was open and as soon as she stepped inside she felt very strange. 'Oh dear, I always look forward to seeing Grandmother, so why do I feel so nervous today?
    'Good Morning?'

But there is no reply. She walks over to the bed and draws back the curtains. Grandmother lies there wearing her night-cap.

Red-Cap 'Oh, Grandmother, what big ears you have.'

Wolf 'The better to hear you with, my sweet.'

Red-Cap 'Oh, Grandmother, what big eyes you have.'

Wolf 'The better to see you with, my love.'

Red-Cap 'Oh, Grandmother, what big hands you have.'

Wolf 'The better to touch you with.'

Red-Cap 'But Grandmother, what a terrible big mouth you have.'

Wolf 'The better to eat you.'

The Wolf gobbles up Red-Cap. Then he drags himself into the bed, falls asleep and starts to snore loudly.

Huntsman The huntsman was just passing the house and thought, 'How loudly the old woman is snoring. I'd better see if something is wrong.'

He goes into the house and when he reaches the bed he sees the Wolf spread out on it.

Huntsman 'So you've come here, you old sinner. I've wanted to catch you for a long, long time.'
He was about to shoot when it flashed through his mind that the wolf might have swallowed the grand-mother whole and that she might still be saved. So he got a good pair of scissors and began to snip the belly of the sleeping wolf. After two snips, he saw the bright red colour of the little red cap. Two snips, three snips, four snips more, and out jumped Little Red-Cap!

Red-Cap 'Oh, how frightened I've been! It's so dark inside the wolf!'

Then out comes Grandmother, hardly breathing but still alive.

Red-Cap Little Red-Cap rushed outside and quickly fetched some big stones and they filled the wolf's belly with them.

When the Wolf wakes up, it tries to run away, but the stones in its stomach are too heavy and it drops down dead.

Red-Cap When the wolf was dead, all three were delighted.

Huntsman The huntsman skinned the wolf and went home with its pelt.

Grandmother The grandmother ate the cake and drank the wine and soon began to feel much better.

Red-Cap And Little Red-Cap promised herself, 'Never so long as I live will I wander off the path into the woods when my mother has warned me not to.'

Clever Hans

Hans Hans' mother said:

Mother 'Where are you off to Hans?'

Hans Hans said, 'To see Gretel.'

Mother 'Behave well, Hans.'

Hans 'Oh, I'll behave well. Goodbye Mother'

Mother 'Goodbye, Hans.'

Hans Hans goes to Gretel. 'Good day, Gretel.'

Gretel 'Good day, Hans. What have you brought that's good?'

Hans 'I've brought nowt. I want to have something given to me.'

Gretel Gretel presents Hans with a needle.

Hans 'Goodbye, Gretel.'

Gretel 'Goodbye, Hans.'

Hans Hans takes the needle, sticks it into a hay cart, follows the cart home. 'Good evening, Mother.'

Mother 'Good evening, Hans. Where have you been?'

Hans 'With Gretel.'

Mother 'What did Gretel give you?'

Hans 'Gave me a needle.'

Mother 'Where is the needle, Hans?'

Hans 'Stuck in the hay-cart.'

Mother 'That was poorly done, Hans. You should have stuck the needle in your vest.'

Hans 'Not to worry. I'll do better next time.'

Mother 'Where are you off to, Hans?'

Hans 'To Gretel's, Mother.'

Mother 'Behave well, Hans.'

Hans 'Oh, I'll behave well. Goodbye, Mother.'

Mother 'Goodbye, Hans.'

Hans Hans goes to Gretel. 'Good day, Gretel.'

Gretel 'Good day, Hans. What have you brought that's good?'

Hans 'I've brought nowt. I want to have something given to me.'

Gretel Gretel presents Hans with a knife.

Hans 'Goodbye, Gretel.'

Gretel 'Goodbye, Hans.'

Hans Hans takes the knife, sticks it in his vest, and goes home. 'Good evening, Mother.'

Mother 'Good evening, Hans. Where have you been?'

Hans 'With Gretel.'

Mother 'What did you take her?'

Hans 'Took nowt. Got given something.'

Mother 'What did Gretel give you?'

Hans 'Gave me a knife.'

Mother 'Where is the knife, Hans?'

Hans 'Stuck in my vest.'

Mother 'That was poorly done, Hans. You should have put the knife in your pocket.'

Hans 'Not to worry. Do better next time.'

Mother 'Where are you off to, Hans?'

Hans 'To Gretel, Mother.'

Mother 'Behave well, Hans.'

Hans 'Oh, I'll behave well. Goodbye, Mother.'

Mother 'Goodbye, Hans.'

Hans Hans goes to Gretel. 'Good day, Gretel.'

Gretel 'Good day, Hans. What good thing have you brought?'

Hans 'I've brought nowt. I want something given me.'

Gretel Gretel presents Hans with a young goat.

Hans 'Goodbye, Gretel.'

Gretel 'Goodbye, Hans.'

Hans Hans takes the goat, ties its legs and puts it in his pocket. When he gets home it has suffocated. 'Good evening, Mother.'

Mother 'Good evening, Hans. Where have you been?'

Hans 'With Gretel.'

Mother 'What did you take her?'

Hans 'Took nowt. Got given something.'

Mother 'What did Gretel give you?'

Hans 'She gave me a goat.'

Mother 'Where is the goat, Hans?'

Hans 'Put it in my pocket.'

Mother 'That was poorly done, Hans. You should have put a rope round the goat's neck.'

Hans 'Not to worry. Do better next time.'

Mother 'Where are you off to, Hans?'

Hans 'To Gretel, Mother.'

Mother 'Behave well, Hans.'

Hans 'Oh. I'll behave well. Goodbye, Mother.'

Mother 'Goodbye, Hans.'

Hans Hans goes to Gretel. 'Good day, Gretel.'

Gretel 'Good day, Hans. What good thing have you brought?'

Hans 'I've brought nowt. I want something given.'

Gretel Gretel presents Hans with a piece of bacon.

Hans 'Goodbye, Gretel.'

Gretel 'Goodbye, Hans.'

Hans Hans takes the bacon, ties it to a rope and drags it away behind him. The dogs come sniffing and scoff the bacon. When he gets home he has the rope in his hand with nothing at the end of it. 'Good evening, Mother.'

Mother 'Good evening, Hans. Where have you been?'

Hans 'With Gretel.'

Mother 'What did you take her?'

Hans 'Took nowt. Got given something.'

Mother 'What did Gretel give you?'

Hans 'Gave me a bit of bacon.'

Mother 'Where is the bacon, Hans?'

Hans 'I tied it to a rope, pulled it home. Dogs had it.'

Mother 'That was poorly done, Hans. You should have carried the bacon on your head.'

Hans 'Not to worry. Do better next time.'

Mother 'Where are you off to, Hans?'

Hans 'To Gretel, Mother.'

Mother 'Behave well, Hans.'

Hans 'Oh, I'll behave well. Goodbye, Mother.'

Mother 'Goodbye, Hans.'

Hans Hans goes to Gretel. 'Good day, Gretel.'

Gretel 'Good day, Hans. What have you brought me that's good?'

Hans 'I've brought nowt. I want something given.'

Gretel Gretel presents Hans with a calf.

Hans 'Goodbye, Gretel.'

Gretel 'Goodbye, Hans.'

Hans Hans takes the calf and puts it on his head. The calf gives his face a kicking. 'Good evening, Mother.'

Mother 'Good evening, Hans. Where have you been?'

Hans 'With Gretel.'

Mother 'What did you take her?'

Hans 'Took nowt. Got given something.'

Mother 'What did Gretel give you?'

Hans 'A calf.'

Mother 'Where is the calf, Hans?'

Hans 'Put it on my head, it kicked my face.'

Mother 'That was poorly done, Hans. You should have led the calf and put it in the stable.'

Hans 'Not to worry. Do better next time.'

Mother 'Where are you off to, Hans?'

Hans 'To Gretel, Mother.'

Mother 'Behave well, Hans.'

Hans 'Oh, I'll behave well. Goodbye, Mother.'

Mother 'Goodbye, Hans.'

Hans Hans goes to Gretel. 'Good day, Gretel.'

Gretel 'Good day, Hans. What good thing have you brought?'

Hans 'Nowt. I want something given.'

Gretel Gretel says to Hans. 'I will come with you.'

Hans Hans takes Gretel, ties her to a rope, leads her to the stable and binds her tight. Then Hans goes to his mother. 'Good evening, Mother.'

Mother 'Good evening, Hans. Where have you been?'

Hans 'With Gretel.'

Mother 'What did you take her?'

Hans 'I took her nowt.'

Mother 'What did Gretel give you?'

Hans 'She gave me nowt. She came back with me.'

Mother 'Where have you left Gretel?'

Hans 'I led her by the rope, tied her up in the stable, and scattered a bit of grass for her.'

Mother 'That was poorly done, Hans. You should have cast warm eyes on her.'

Hans 'Not to worry. Will do better.'
   Hans marched into the stable, cut out all the calves' and sheep's eyes, and threw them in Gretel's face.

Gretel Then Gretel became very angry, tore herself loose and ran away.

All Except for Hans Gretel was no longer the bride of Hans.

The Hare and the Hedgehog

Narrator This tale, my splendid listeners, may seem to you to be false, but it really is true, because I heard it from my grandfather, and when he told it he always said, 'It must be true, my dear, or else no one could tell it to you.' This is the story.

One Sunday morning around harvest time, just as the buckwheat was blooming, the sun was shining, the breeze was blowing, the larks were singing, the bees were buzzing, the folk were off to church in their Sunday best, everything that lived was happy and the hedgehog was happy too.

The hedgehog was stood by his own front door, arms akimbo, relishing the morning and singing a song to himself half-aloud. It was no better or worse a song than the songs which hedgehogs usually sing on a Sabbath morning. His wife was inside, washing and drying the children, and he suddenly decided that he'd take a stroll in the field and see how his turnips were doing.

The Hedgehog sets off for the field.

Narrator He hadn't gone very far, and was just turning round the sloe-bush which grows outside the field, to go up into the turnip-field, when he noticed the hare. The hare was out and about on a similar errand to visit his cabbages. The hedgehog called out a friendly good morning.

Hedgehog 'Good morning!'

Narrator But the hare, a distinguished gentleman in his own way, was hoity-toity and gave the hedgehog a snooty look.

Hare 'What brings you scampering about in the field so early in the morning?'

Hedgehog 'I'm taking a walk.'

Hare 'A walk! Surely you can think of a better use for those legs of yours.'

Narrator These words made the hedgehog livid with rage, for he couldn't bear any reference to his legs, which are naturally crooked.

Hedgehog 'You seem to think you can do more with your legs than I can with mine.'

Hare 'That's exactly what I think.'

Hedgehog 'That can soon be put to the test. I'll wager that if we run a race, I shall beat you.'

Hare 'That's preposterous! With those hedgehoggy legs! Well, I'm perfectly willing if you have such an absurd fancy for it. What shall we wager?'

Hedgehog 'A golden sovereign and a bottle of brandy.'

Hare 'Done. Shake hands on it. We might as well do it at once.'

Hedgehog 'Nay, nay, there's no rush. I'm going home for some breakfast. I'll be back at this spot in half-an-hour.'

Narrator The hare was quite satisfied with this, so the hedgehog set off home.

Hedgehog 'The hare is betting on his long legs, but I'll get the better of him. He may be an important gentleman, but he's a foolish fellow and he'll pay for what he's said.'

The Hedgehog arrives back home and calls his Wife.

Hedgehog 'Wife, dress yourself quickly. You've got to come up to the field with me.'

18

Wife 'What's going on?'

Hedgehog 'I've made a wager with the hare for a gold sovereign and a bottle of brandy, and we have to race each other. You must be there.'

Wife 'Husband, are you not right in the head? Have you completely lost your wits? What are you thinking of, running a race with the hare?'

Hedgehog 'Hold your tongue, woman, that's my affair. Don't try to discuss things which are matters for men. Now get yourself dressed and come with me.'

Narrator What else was the wife of a hedgehog to do? She had to obey him, like it or like it not.

They set off towards the field.

Hedgehog 'Pay attention to what I'm saying. The long field will be our race-course. I'll run in one furrow and the hare in the other. We'll start from the top. You position yourself at the bottom of the furrow. When the hare arrives at the end of the furrow next to you, just shout out "I'm here already".'

Narrator The hedgehog showed his wife her place, then walked up top to meet the hare.

Hare 'Shall we start then?'

Hedgehog 'Ready when you are.'

Hare 'Then both at once.'

Narrator The hare counted . . .

Hare 'Once. Twice. Thrice and Away!'

Narrator . . . And flew off at the speed of arrogance down the field. But the hedgehog only ran three steps, then crouched down, quiet and sleekit in his furrow.

As soon as the hare arrived full pelt at the bottom of the field, the hedgehog's wife was already there saying . . .

Wife 'I'm here already.'

Narrator The hare was flabbergasted. He thought it really was the hedgehog because the wife looked just like her husband.

Hare 'This hasn't been done fairly. We must run again. Let us do it again.'

Narrator And a second time he whooshed off like a whirlwind. But the hedgehog's wife stayed modestly in her place and when the hare reached the other end of the field, there was the hedgehog himself crying out . . .

Hedgehog 'I'm here already!'

The Hare becomes furious.

Hare 'Again! Again! We must run it again!'

Hedgehog 'Fine. I'm happy to run as often as you choose.'

The Hare tears off again, but each time the Hedgehog tricks him. Every time the Hare reaches one end of the field, the Hedgehog or his Wife says:

Hedgehog and **Wife** 'I'm here already.'

Narrator The hare ran another seventy-three times. But at the seventy-fourth time, the hare couldn't make it to the end. He collapsed in the middle of the field and a ribbon of blood streamed from his mouth. The hare was dead. The hedgehog ran up and took the gold sovereign which he had won and the bottle of brandy. He called his wife out of the furrow and the pair of them strolled home on their eight legs in great delight. If they're not dead, they're still living there.

Snow White

Narrator In the cold heart of winter, when snow fell as though the white sky had been torn into a million pieces, a Queen sat by a window sewing. The frame of the window was made of black ebony. And while the Queen was sewing and looking out at the snow, she pricked her finger with the needle and three drops of blood fell upon the snow. The red looked so pretty against the white, that the Queen suddenly thought to herself . . .

Mother and **Chorus** 'I wish I had a child as white as snow, as red as blood and as black as the wood on the window-frame.'

Narrator Soon after that, she had a little daughter who was as white as snow, with lips as red as blood and hair as black as ebony. She was called Snow White and when she was born, the Queen died.

After a year had gone by, the King married again. His new wife was a beautiful woman, but she was proud and vain and couldn't bear the thought of anyone else being more beautiful. She owned a wonderful mirror and when she stood before it, looking at her reflection, and said:

Queen
   'Mirror, mirror on the wall,
   Who in this land is fairest of all?'

Narrator The mirror replied:
   'You are, Queen. Fairest of all.'

Queen Then she was pleased because she knew the mirror always told the truth.

Narrator But Snow White was growing up, and becoming more and more beautiful. And when she was seven years old she was as lovely as the day and ever, and more beautiful than the Queen herself. One day, the Queen asked her mirror:

Queen
'Mirror, mirror on the wall,
Who in this land is fairest of all?'

Narrator And the mirror answered:
'Queen, you are beautiful, day and night,
But even more lovely is little Snow White.'

Queen Then the Queen got a shock. From that moment, whenever she looked at Snow White, her heart turned sour in her breast she hated her so much. Envy and pride crept and coiled round her heart like ugly weeds, so that she could get no peace night or day.

Narrator One day she called a huntsman and said:

Queen 'Take the girl into the forest. I want her out of my sight. Kill her – and fetch me back her lungs and liver to prove it.'

The Huntsman does what she says and takes Snow White away. He pulls out his knife to stab her heart.

Snow White 'Please, dear Huntsman, spare my life! I will run away into the wild woods and never come back.'

As she is so beautiful, the Huntsman takes pity on her.

Huntsman 'Poor child. Run away then. The wild beasts will eat you soon enough.'

Narrator A young boar ran by and he slaughtered it, cut out its lungs and liver and took them to the Queen to prove the girl was dead. The cook had to salt, simmer and serve them, and the Queen ate them up and thought she'd eaten Snow White's lungs and liver.

Snow White was alone in the forest and terrified. She began to run over stones as sharp as envy, through thorns as cruel as long fingernails. Wild beasts ran past her but did her no harm. She ran as long as her feet could carry her, until it was almost evening. It was then that she saw a little cottage and went into it to rest.

Snow White Everything in the cottage was small, but neater and cleaner than can be told. There was a white wooden table and seven little plates, each with a little spoon. There were seven little knives and forks and seven little tankards.

She eats a morsel of bread and vegetables from each plate and sips a swallow of wine from each mug.

Snow White Against the wall were seven little beds side by side, each one covered with a snow-white eiderdown. But one was too narrow, one too short, one too soft, one too hard, one too lumpy, one too smooth . . .

Narrator But the seventh was just right, so she snuggled down in it, said a prayer, and went to sleep.

When it is dark, the owners of the cottage come back. They are Seven Dwarfs who work in the mountains digging for gold and copper.
They light their seven candles to fill the cottage with light and at once they see that someone has been there.

Dwarf 1 'Who's been sitting in my chair?'

Dwarf 2 'Who's been eating off my plate?'

Dwarf 3 'Who's had some of my bread?'

Dwarf 4 'Who's been biting my vegetables?'

Dwarf 5 'Who's been using my fork?'

Dwarf 6 'Who's been cutting with my knife?'

The First Dwarf goes over to his bed.

Dwarf 1 'Who's been lying on my bed?'

The other Dwarfs go to their beds.

Dwarfs 'Somebody's been getting into my bed too!'

The Seventh Dwarf finds Snow White asleep on his bed.

Dwarf 7 'Over here!'

The Dwarfs crowd around the bed and gaze down at Snow White.

Dwarfs 'Oh goodness! Oh mercy! What a beautiful child.'

Narrator/Dwarf 7 They were so pleased that they let her sleep peacefully on. The seventh dwarf slept with his companions, one hour with each, and so passed the night, and was glad to do so.

Snow White When morning came, Snow White awoke and was frightened when she saw the seven dwarfs. But they were friendly and asked her her name. 'My name is Snow White.'

Dwarf 2 'How have you come to our house?'

Snow White She told them how her step-mother had ordered her to be killed, but that the huntsman had taken pity on her and she had run through the forest for a whole day until she arrived at their little cottage.

Dwarf 6 'If you will take care of our house.'

Dwarf 5 'Make the beds.'

Dwarf 3 'Set the table.'

Dwarf 4 'Keep everything neat and tidy.'

Dwarf 1 'Cook, wash, sew.'

Dwarf 7 'Knit and mend.'

Dwarf 2 'You can stay here with us and you shall want for nothing.'

Snow White 'With all my heart!'

As the Dwarfs are leaving.

Dwarf 6 'Beware of your step-mother.'

Dwarf 3 'She will soon find out you are here.'

Dwarfs 'Don't let anyone into the house.'

Narrator But the Queen believed that she'd eaten the lungs Snow White breathed with, and that once again she was more beautiful than anyone. She went to her mirror and said:

Queen
'Who in this land is the fairest of all?'

Narrator/Mirror
'Queen, you're the fairest I can see.
But deep in the wood where seven dwarfs dwell,
Snow White is still alive and well
And you are not so fair as she.'

Queen Then the Queen was appalled because she knew that the mirror never lied and that the huntsman had tricked her. She stained her face and dressed up like an old pedlar-woman, so that not even her own mirror would have known her. In this disguise she made her way to the house of the seven dwarfs.

Disguised Queen 'Pretty things for sale, very cheap, very cheap.'

Snow White 'Good day, pedlar-woman, what are you selling today?'

Disguised Queen 'Beautiful things, pretty things, fair things, skirt-laces of all colours.'

She pulls out a lace of brightly coloured silk.

Snow White I can let this friendly old woman in.

She unlocks the door and lets the Disguised Queen in.

Disguised Queen 'Child, what a sight you are! Come here and let the old pedlar-woman lace you properly for once.'

Snow White lets herself be laced with the new laces. But the Queen laces so quickly and viciously and tightly that Snow White loses her breath and falls down as if dead.

Queen 'Now I am the most beautiful!'

The Disguised Queen hurries away.

Narrator Soon afterwards, when evening fell, the seven dwarfs came home – but how distressed they were to see their dear little Snow White lying on the ground. They lifted her up and, when they saw she was laced too tightly, they cut the laces. Then Snow White started to breathe a little and after a while came back to life. When the dwarfs heard what had happened, they said:

Dwarf 1 'The old pedlar-woman was no one else but the evil Queen.'

Dwarf 3 'Be careful.'

Dwarf 4 'Let nobody in when we are not with you.'

Queen The Queen ran home and went straight to her mirror:

'Mirror, mirror, on the wall
Who in this land is fairest of all?'

Narrator
'Deep in the wood where seven dwarfs dwell,
Snow White is still alive and well.
Although you're the fairest I can see,
Queen, you are not so fair as she.'

The Queen is filled with fear.

Queen 'Now I will think of something that will really rid me of you for ever.' And so she made a poisonous comb.

She disguises herself as another old woman and makes her way back to the Seven Dwarfs' house.

Disguised Queen 'Good things for sale, cheap, cheap.'

Snow White 'Go away, please. I can't let anyone in.'

Disguised Queen 'You can at least look.'

Snow White eventually opens the door and lets the Disguised Queen in.

Disguised Queen 'Now I'll comb your ebony hair properly for once.'

As soon as the comb is in Snow White's hair, she falls to the ground as if dead.

Queen and **Disguised Queen** 'You prize beauty. You are nothing now.'

When the Seven Dwarfs arrive home, they see Snow White on the ground. They find the poisoned comb and Snow White comes to herself as soon as it is removed. The Dwarfs once again warn her to be on her guard and to open the door to no one.

Meanwhile the Queen goes home to face her mirror.

Queen
'Mirror, mirror, on the wall,
Who in this land is fairest of all?'

Narrator/Mirror and **Chorus**
'Queen, you're the fairest I can see.
But deep in the woods where seven dwarfs dwell,
Snow White is still alive and well
And no one's as beautiful as she.'

Queen 'Snow White shall die, even if it costs me my life!'
She went into a quiet, secret, lonely room where no
one ever came, and there she made a very poisonous
apple.

Narrator On the outside it looked pretty – crisp and
white with a blood-red cheek, so that everyone who saw
it longed for it – but whoever ate a piece of the red cheek
would die.

*She paints her face, disguising herself as a farmer's
wife, and goes again to the house of the Seven
Dwarfs. She knocks at the door and Snow White puts
her head out of the window.*

Snow White 'I can't let anyone in. The seven dwarfs
have forbidden me.'

Disguised Queen 'It's all the same to me, dear. I'll soon
get rid of my apples. Here – you can have one.'

Snow White 'No, I dare not take anything.'

Disguised Queen 'Are you afraid it might be poisoned?
Look, I'll cut the apple in two pieces, you eat the red
cheek and I will eat the white.'

*But only the red cheek is poisoned. Snow White longs
for the apple, and when she sees the farmer's wife sink*

her teeth into it, she can't resist any more and
stretches out her hand and takes the poisonous half.
She takes a bite and dies.

Queen and **Disguised Queen**
'Snow White,
Blood Red,
Black as Coffin Wood –
This time the seven dwarfs
Will find you dead for good.'

The Queen hurries home and goes to her mirror.

Queen
'Mirror, mirror on the wall,
Who in this land is fairest of all?'

After a while the mirror answers.

Narrator/Mirror
'Oh, Queen, in this land you are fairest of all.'

Narrator When the dwarfs came home in the evening,
they found Snow White. She breathed no longer and was
dead. They lifted her up and looked for anything
poisonous, unlaced her, combed her hair, washed her in
water and wine, but it was all useless. The girl was dead
and stayed dead. So the seven of them sat round and for
three whole days they wept for Snow White.

Then they were going to bury her, but she still looked
so alive with her pretty red cheeks. They said, 'We
cannot put her in the cold, dark earth.' So they had a
coffin of glass made, so that she could be seen from all
sides. They laid her in it and wrote her name on it in
gold letters and put that she was daughter of a King.
They placed the coffin up on the mountain and one of
them always guarded it. Birds came, too, to weep for
Snow White. First an owl, then a raven and last a dove.

And now Snow White lay for a very long time in her

glass coffin as though she were only sleeping; still as white as snow, as red as blood, and with hair as black as ebony.

Prince It happened, though, that a King's son came to the forest and went to the dwarfs' house to spend the night. He saw the coffin glinting like a mirror on the mountain, and he saw Snow White inside it and read what was written there in letters of gold. He said to the dwarfs, 'Let me have the coffin. I will give you anything you name for it.'

Narrator But the dwarfs answered that they wouldn't part with it for all the treasure in the world.

Prince 'Let me have it as a gift. My heart cannot beat without seeing Snow White. I will honour and cherish her above all else in this world.'

Narrator Because he spoke like this, the dwarfs pitied him and gave him the coffin.

The King's son had it carried away on his servants' shoulders. As they did this, they tripped over some tree-roots, and with the jolt the piece of poisonous apple which Snow White had swallowed came out of her throat.

Snow White opens her eyes and sits up.

Snow White 'Heavens, where am I?'

Prince 'You are with me.'

He told her what had happened and said, 'I love you more than my heart can hold. Come with me to my father's palace. Be my wife.'

Snow White Snow White was willing and did go with him.

Prince And their wedding was held with great show and splendour.

Narrator Snow White's step-mother was bidden to the feast.

Queen When she was dressed in her best jewels and finery, she danced to her mirror and queried:
    'Mirror, mirror, on the wall
    Who in this land is fairest of all?'

Narrator/Mirror
    'You are the old Queen. That much is true.
    But the new young Queen is fairer than you.'

Queen Then the Queen cursed and swore and was so demented, so wretched, so distraught, that she could hardly think. At first, she wouldn't go to the feast; but she had no peace, and had to see the young Queen. So she went.

Narrator And when she walked in she saw that it was Snow White and was unable to move with fear and rage. She stood like a statue of hate.

Snow White But iron dancing shoes were already heating in the fire. They were brought in with tongs and set before her. Then she was forced to put on the red-hot shoes and she was made to dance, dance, until she dropped down dead.

The Musicians of Bremen

Man A man had a donkey . . .

Donkey Who had worked hard for years carrying heavy sacks of corn to the mill.

Man But the donkey's strength had gone and he was getting more and more unfit for the job.
   So the man was thinking how he could get shut of him and save the expense of feeding him.

The Man starts to load his gun.

Donkey But the donkey got wind of this and ran away. He set off towards Bremen and thought he might try his luck at being a town-musician. After a while on the road, he came across a Hound-Dog lying by the roadside, panting away as though he'd run very hard. 'Hello, old Hound-Dog, what are you gasping like that for?'

Dog 'Ah, I'm not getting any younger and get weaker every day so I can't hunt any more. My master was going to kill me, so I ran away. But how shall I make my living now?'

Donkey 'I'll tell you what. I'm on my way to Bremen to become a town-musician. Why don't you come with me? I'll play the lute and you can play away the kettle-drum!'

Dog The hound was pleased with this idea.

Donkey and **Dog** And so on they went.

Donkey Before long, they found a cat slumped by the roadside.

Dog With a face like three wet Wednesdays.

Donkey 'Now then, old Lick-Whiskers, what makes you look so miserable?'

Cat 'How else should I look with my problems? Just because I'm getting on and my teeth are worn to stumps and I prefer to sit dreaming by the fire rather than run about after mice, my mistress wants to drown me. So I've run away. But now, who's to tell me what to do and where to go?'

Donkey 'Come with us to Bremen to be a town-musician. You're well-known for your caterwauling music of the night!'

Cat The cat was impressed with this plan.

Donkey, Dog and **Cat** And on the three of them went.

Cock Lala, lala, lala! Lala, lala, lala!

Donkey Quite soon our three runaways came to a farm and there on the gate perched a cockerel crowing like mad.

Cock Lala, lala, lala! Lala, lala, lala!

Donkey 'That terrible crowing's going right through us. What on earth's up?'

Cock 'I'm forecasting fine weather, because today's wash-day in Heaven and Our Lady wants to dry Baby Jesus's tiny shirts. But they've got guests coming here for dinner tomorrow, and that callous, hard-hearted house-keeper has told cook to cook me. I've to have my head chopped off tonight, so I'm having having a good crow while I can. Lala, lala, lala!'

Donkey 'Preposterous, Redcomb! Come instead with us to Bremen. You'll be better there than in a casserole.

With that voice of yours and our rhythm, we're going to make music the like of which has never been heard!'

Cock The cock thought this seemed an excellent plan.

Donkey, Dog, Cat and **Cock** And all four of them went on their way together.

Donkey Bremen town was too far to reach in a day, though, and in the evening they reached a forest – where they decided to spend the night. The donkey . . .

Dog And the dog . . .

Donkey Lay down under a large tree.

Cat The cat settled himself in the branches.

Cock And the cock flew right to the top and perched there. Before he went to sleep, he looked to north, south, east and west and thought he spied a quaver of light in the distance. So he called down to his fellow-musicians that there must be a house nearby for him to see a light.

Donkey 'Then let's go and find it. The accommodation here's appalling.'

Dog 'I wouldn't turn up my nose at a plate of bones with some meat on them.'

Cock So they set off in the direction of the light . . . Which got bigger and brighter and more attractive, until they came to a well-lit house.

Donkey The donkey, who was the biggest, sneaked up to the window and peeped in.

Cock 'What can you see, old Greymule?'

Donkey 'What can I see! Only a table groaning with wonderful things to eat and drink and a band of robbers sat round it filling their boots!'

Cock 'Those words are music to my ears! That's the kind of thing we're after.'

Dog and **Cat** 'Yes, yes! If only we were inside!'

Donkey, Dog, Cat and **Cock** So the four famished fugitives put their furry or feathery heads together to decide how to get rid of the robbers. At last they thought of a plan.

Donkey Old Greymule was to stand on his hind-legs with his forefeet on the window.

Dog Old Hound-Dog was to jump on the donkey's back.

Cat Old Lick-Whiskers was to climb on the back of the dog.

Cock And lastly Redcomb was to fly up and perch on the head of the cat, like a hat.

> *When they finally manage this, the Donkey gives a signal, and they launch into their music. The Donkey brays, the Hound howls, the Cat caterwauls and the Cock crows. For an encore, they crash into the room through the window, smashing the glass and still singing. The Robbers run away.*

Cock Once the robbers had fled freaked into the forest, the four friends sat down at the table, well pleased with what was left, and feasted as though they wouldn't see food and drink for a fortnight.

When they had finished their meal, they put out the light and found somewhere comfortable to sleep, each according to his needs and nature.

Donkey The donkey dossed down in the shit-heap in the yard.

Dog The hound hunched down behind the door.

Cat The cat curled up near the ashes on the hearth.

Cock And the cock flapped up to roost in the rafters. They were all so tired after their long journey that they soon fell fast asleep.

Chief Robber The robbers were watching the house from a safe distance. When midnight had passed, and they saw that the light was out and all was quiet, their captain said: 'Well, now. Perhaps we shouldn't have let ourselves be frightened off so easily.' He ordered one of his band to go back to the house and investigate.

Second Robber The robber found everything as silent and dark as a closed piano-lid, as hushed as drowned bag-pipers. She fetched a candle from the kitchen and thought she saw two glowing coals in the fire and stuck her candle in them to light it . . .

The Cat howls and flies at his face, scratching and spitting. The man, terrified out of his wits, runs for the back door – but he treads on the Dog, which leaps up and bites him on the leg. He runs into the yard and is about to leap over the shit-heap when he receives a kick in the backside from the Donkey. At all the commotion, the Cock wakes up:

Cock 'Cock a doodle do! Cock a doodle do!'

The Robber runs back to his band and says to the Chief Robber:

Robber 'Oh, my God! There's a horrible witch in the house. I felt her ratty breath and her long claws on my face. Oh God! There's a man with a knife by the back door who stabbed me in the leg. Oh! There's a black monster in the yard who beat me with a wooden club. God! And to top it all, there's a judge on the roof and he called out, "That's the crook that'll do! The crook that'll do!" So I got out of there as fast as I could.'

Chief Robber After that, the robbers didn't dare go back to the house.

Cock But the four talented members of the Bremen Town Band liked the house so much that they just stayed on. And they're still there.

Donkey This story has been told for years. The mouth of the last person to tell this tale still has a warm tongue in it – as you can see.

The four animals stick their tongues out at the audience.

Rumpelstiltskin

Miller There was a miller once who was very poor, but he had one daughter more beautiful than any treasure. It happened one day that he came to speak to the King and to make himself look special he said, 'I have a daughter who can spin straw into gold.'

King 'That's a talent that would please me hugely. If your daughter is as clever as you say, bring her to my palace tomorrow and I'll put her to the test.'

When the girl was brought to him, the King led her to a room that was full of straw. He gave her a spinning-wheel.

'Set to work. You have all night ahead of you. But if you haven't spun all this straw into gold by dawn, you must die.' Then he locked the door with his own hands . . .

Daughter And left her there alone. The poor miller's daughter sat there without a clue what to do. She had no idea how to spin straw into gold and she grew more and more frightened and started to cry.

Suddenly the door opens and a little man enters.

Rumpelstiltskin 'Good evening, Mistress Miller, why are you crying?'

Daughter 'Oh, I have to spin this straw into gold and I don't know how to do it.'

Rumpelstiltskin 'What will you give me if I do it for you?'

Daughter 'My necklace.'

Rumpelstiltskin 'Done.'

Daughter The little man took the necklace, squatted down before the spinning-wheel, and whirr, whirr, whirr! Three turns and the bobbin was full.

Rumpelstiltskin And so he went on all night and at sunrise all the bobbins were full of gold.

King First thing in the morning, in came the King and when he saw all the gold he was amazed and delighted. But the gold-greed grew in his heart and so he took the miller's daughter to an even bigger room filled up with straw and told her to spin the lot into gold if she valued her life.

Rumpelstiltskin 'What will you give me if I spin all this straw into gold?'

Daughter 'The ring from my finger.'

Rumpelstiltskin So the little man took the ring and whirred away at the wheel all the long dark night and by dawn each dull strand of straw was glistening gold.

King The King was beside himself with pleasure at the treasure. He took the miller's daughter to an even larger room full of straw and told her, 'You must spin all of this into gold tonight and if you succeed you shall be my wife.'

As soon as the girl is alone, the little man appears for the third time.

Rumpelstiltskin 'What will you give me this time if I spin the straw into gold for you?'

Daughter 'I have nothing left to give.'

Rumpelstiltskin 'Then you must promise to give me the first child you have after you are Queen.'

Daughter 'Who knows what the future holds . . . ' As she had no choice, she gave her word to the little man.

He starts to spin until all the straw is gold.

King When the King arrived in the morning he saw everything just as he wished. He held the wedding at once.

King and **Chorus** And the miller's beautiful daughter became a Queen.

Queen After a year she brought a gorgeous golden child into the world and thought no more of the little man.

Rumpelstiltskin But one day he stepped suddenly into her room. 'Now give me what you promised.'

Queen The Queen was truly horrified and offered him all the gold and riches of the kingdom if he would only leave the child.

Rumpelstiltskin 'No. I'd rather have a living child than all the treasure in the world.'

The Queen sobs bitterly. Eventually the little man takes pity on her.

Rumpelstiltskin 'I'll give you three days. If you can find out my name by then, you can keep your child.'

Queen The Queen sat up all night, searching her brains for his name like someone sieving for gold. She went through every single name she could think of. She sent out a messenger to ask everywhere in the land for all the names that could be found. On the next day, when the little man came, she recited the whole alphabet of names that she'd learned, starting with Balthasar, Casper, Melchior . . .

Rumpelstiltskin But to each one the little man said, 'That isn't my name.'

Queen On the second day, she sent servants all round the neighbourhood to find more names and she tried all the strange and unusual ones on the little man. 'Perhaps you're called Shortribs or Sheepshanks or Lacelegs.'

Rumpelstiltskin 'That isn't my name.'

Queen On the third day, the messenger came back and said:

Messenger 'I haven't managed to find a single new name, but as I approached a high mountain at the end of the forest, the place where fox and hare bid each other goodnight, I saw a small hut. There was a fire burning outside it and round the fire danced an absurd little man. He hopped on one leg and bawled:

Messenger and **Rumpelstiltskin**
  'Bake today! Tomorrow brew!
  Then I'll take the Queen's child!
  She will cry and wish she knew
  That RUMPELSTILTSKIN's how I'm styled!'

The Queen is delighted. But then the little man enters:

Rumpelstiltskin 'Well, Mistress Queen, what is my name?'

Queen 'Is it Tom?'

Rumpelstiltskin 'No.'

Queen 'Is it Dick?'

Rumpelstiltskin 'No.'

Queen 'Is it Harry?'

Rumpelstiltskin 'No.'

Queen 'Perhaps your name is Rumpelstiltskin?'

Rumpelstiltskin 'The devil has told you! The devil has told you!'

In his fury he stamped his right foot so hard on the ground that it went right in up to his waist.

Queen And then in a rage he pulled at his left leg so hard that he tore himself in two.

Brother Scamp

Scamp Once there was a great war and when it was over many soldiers were discharged. One of these was Brother Scamp.

He was given one loaf of ammunition-bread and four shillings and sent on his way.

Peter St Peter, however, had disguised himself as a beggarman and was sitting by the roadside. When Brother Scamp came along, he begged for charity.

Scamp 'Dear beggarman, what am I to give you? I have been a soldier, but on my dismissal I was given only this loaf of ammunition-bread and four shillings. Once they've gone, I shall have to beg myself. Even so, I'll give you something.' Then Brother Scamp divided his loaf into four parts, gave one to the beggarman, and gave him a shilling as well.

Peter The apostle thanked him and hurried on his way; but further along the road he sat down again disguised as a different beggar.

When Brother Scamp comes along, he begs for a gift as before.

Scamp Brother Scamp spoke as he had earlier but again gave him a piece of bread and a shilling.

Peter St Peter thanked him and went on, but for the third time sat down in Brother Scamp's path.

Peter begs again. Brother Scamp gives him another quarter of bread and another shilling. St Peter thanks him as before.

Scamp Brother Scamp, with only one shilling and the last morsel of bread left, went on to an inn where he ate the bread and ordered a shilling's worth of ale.

When he had finished, he set off once more.

Peter And St Peter, this time dressed up as a discharged soldier, met him again. 'Good day, comrade. Can you spare a bit of bread and a shilling for some beer?'

Scamp 'Where would I find them? I've been discharged and all the army gave me was a loaf of ammunition-bread and four shillings. I met three beggars on the road and I gave each of them a quarter of bread and a shilling. I ate the last quarter of bread at an inn and spent the last shilling on ale. So now my pockets are empty. If you're in the same boat, then let us go begging together.'

Peter 'There's no need to do that. I know a bit about healing. I'll soon earn as much as I need from that. Just come along with me, and if I make any money at it you can have half.'

Scamp 'Fair enough.' And the two soldiers went on their way together.

They soon came to a peasant's house, inside which they heard loud weeping and cries of lamentation. They went in. A man lay there, very sick and at death's door, and his poor wife was wailing her lungs out.

Peter 'Stop your weeping and wailing. I will make this man well again.'

Scamp He took some ointment from his pocket and healed the man quicker than an angel's wing. The man stood up in the best of health.

The Husband and Wife are overjoyed.

Wife 'How can we thank you?'

Husband 'What can we give you to repay you?'

46

Peter But St Peter wouldn't accept any reward; and the more the peasant folk offered, the more he refused.

Brother Scamp nudges St Peter.

Scamp 'Take something, for God's sake. We need it!'

Peter Finally, the woman brought in a lamb and told St Peter that he really must take it.

St Peter still refuses. Scamp gives him a poke.

Scamp 'Take it, take it. We need it.'

Peter (*finally*) 'All right, I'll accept it. But I won't carry it. If you want it so much, then you can carry it.'

Scamp 'Fair enough.'

Scamp hoists the lamb on to his shoulder.

Peter They journeyed on together and came to a forest.

By now Scamp is struggling under the weight of the lamb.

Scamp 'Look, this is a good spot. Let's stop and cook the lamb and eat it.'

Peter 'If you like, but I don't know anything about cooking. If you want to cook, there's a pot. I shall go for a walk until it's ready. But you mustn't start eating until I return. I will come back at the right time.'

Scamp 'Off you go, I'm a nifty hand at cooking. Just leave everything to me.'
Brother Scamp butchered the lamb, lit the fire, threw the meat into the pot and cooked it. When the meat was ready, his comrade hadn't returned, so he removed the meat from the pot, cut it up, and found the heart. 'That's supposed to be the best part.'

He tastes a little bit, then a little bit more, and a little

47

bit more, and soon he eats it all up. Eventually St Peter comes back.

Peter 'You can eat the whole lamb yourself. Just give me the heart.'

Brother Scamp takes a knife and fork and pretends to look for the heart. He pokes and prods anxiously around the flesh and finally gives up.

Scamp 'There isn't any heart.'

Peter 'How is that possible?'

Scamp 'Search me. But hang on a minute! What fools we are! Everyone knows that a lamb hasn't got a heart.'

Peter 'Let's go then. If there's no heart, I don't want any lamb. You can have it all for yourself.'

Scamp 'What I can't eat now, I'll take away in my knapsack.'

He eats up half the lamb and then packs the rest into his knapsack.

Peter They went on their way and after a while St Peter arranged for a great stream of water to block their path. 'You go first!'

Scamp 'No, you go first, comrade . . . If the water proves too deep for him, I can stay behind.'

Peter St Peter waded across and the water only came up to his knees. So Brother Scamp followed him, but the water got deeper and deeper until it was up to his neck.

Scamp 'Brother! Help me!'

Peter 'Confess you ate the lamb's heart!'

Scamp 'No! I didn't eat it!'

48

The water grows even deeper until it is up to his mouth.

Scamp 'Brother! Help me!'

Peter 'Admit you ate the lamb's heart!'

Scamp 'No! I didn't eat it!'

Peter But St Peter would not have the man drown, so he made the water go down and helped him across.

They took to the road again and came to a kingdom where they heard that the King's daughter was ill and on the verge of death.

Scamp 'Now then, Brother! This looks like just the thing for us. If we can cure her, we'll be set up for life!'

Peter St Peter agreed, but walked too slowly for Brother Scamp's liking.

Scamp 'Come on, Brother, hurry up. We want to get there before it's too late.'

Peter But the more Brother Scamp pushed and prodded, the slower St Peter went; and before long they heard that the Princess had died.

Scamp 'I knew it! This is what comes of your dawdling along.'

Peter 'Hold your tongue. I don't just heal sick people. I can make dead people live again.'

Scamp 'Well, if that's the case, make sure we get a decent reward. Ask for half the kingdom at least.'

They went to the Royal Palace where everyone was distraught with grief.

Peter St Peter went straight to the King and vowed to him that he would bring his daughter back to life.

King He was taken to her room and said:

Peter 'Bring me a cauldron of water.' They brought the water and he told everyone to leave the room except for Brother Scamp.

Scamp He cut off the dead girl's limbs and tossed them into the water. He made a fire under the cauldron and boiled them. When all the flesh had fallen off, he took the clean white bones out of the water, placed them on a table, and arranged them in the correct order.

When he has done all this to his satisfaction, he steps forward and says three times:

Peter 'In the name of the Holy Trinity, dead Princess, stand up and live again.'

At the third time, the girl stands up, warm and healthy and beautiful. The King is shaking with joy and gratitude.

King 'Name your reward. Even if you ask for half my kingdom you shall have it.'

Peter 'I want nothing.'

Scamp 'Oh, you cabbage-head!'

He nudges St Peter in the ribs.

Scamp 'Don't be so stupid. You might not want a reward, but I do.'

Peter St Peter still wanted nothing.

King But the King saw that the other man felt quite the opposite and ordered his treasurer to fill Brother Scamp's knapsack with gold.

Peter Again they went on their way. Soon they came to a forest.

Peter 'Now we'll share out the gold.'

Scamp 'Fair enough.'

Peter St Peter divided the gold into three parts.

Scamp 'What nonsense has he got into his head now? Why divide the gold into three when there's only two of us?'

Peter 'I've split the gold perfectly. One part for me, one for you, and one for whoever ate the lamb's heart.'

Scamp 'That was me!'

He scoops up two portions of gold.

Scamp 'I give you my word.'

Peter 'How is that possible, when we know that a lamb has no heart?'

Scamp 'What are you on about, Brother? Everyone knows a lamb has a heart just like any other animal. Why on earth shouldn't it?'

Peter 'Very well, keep the gold for yourself. I have had enough of your company and I'm going on by myself.'

Scamp 'If that's what you want then fair enough, Brother. Goodbye.'

I'm glad to see the back of him . . . What a strange individual he turned out to be.

He now had plenty of money, but he didn't know how to use it sensibly. He squandered some, gave some away, and after a while he was penniless once more. He came to a land where he was told that the King's daughter had died. He thought to himself, 'Hang about! There might be something in this for me. I'll bring her back to life and make sure I get a decent reward.' So he went straight to the King and offered to return his daughter from the dead.

Brother Scamp requests a cauldron of water and orders everyone from the room. He severs the dead girl's limbs, tosses them into the water, and lights a fire exactly as he has seen St Peter do. The water bubbles up. When the flesh falls away from the bones, he takes them out and lays them on the table; but he has no idea of the correct order and gets the bones all jumbled up. Nevertheless, he steps up to the table and cries:

Scamp 'In the name of the Holy Trinity, rise from the dead.'

He says it three times, but not a bone budges. He says it three times more, but it is useless.

Scamp 'Blasted girl! Get up off that table or I'll half-kill you!'

As soon as the words have left his mouth, St Peter comes in through the window, once again disguised as a discharged soldier.

Peter 'Blasphemous, godless man! What are you doing? How can the poor girl rise again when you've got her bones in such a mess?'

Scamp 'I've done the best I could, Brother.'

Peter 'I'll help you out just this once, but if you ever try anything like this again, Heaven help you. Furthermore, you are neither to demand nor accept any reward at all from the King.'

St Peter arranges the bones in the right order and says three times:

Peter 'In the name of the Holy Trinity, rise from the dead.'

The King's daughter breathes and gets up, as healthy

52

and beautiful as ever. St Peter goes out through the window.

Scamp 'That bloke's not the full shilling. What he gives with one hand he takes away with the other. It's beyond me!'

Second King The King offered Brother Scamp any reward he wanted.

Scamp He refused, as he'd been ordered to; but with hints, winks, nudges, shuffles and shrugs, he got the King to fill his knapsack with gold and off he went.

Peter 'Just look at you! Didn't I forbid you to accept anything? And yet out you march as bold as brass with your knapsack bulging with gold.'

Scamp 'I can't help it if they forced it on me.'

Peter 'You'd better not try this sort of thing again or you'll wish you hadn't.'

Scamp 'Have no fear on that score, Brother. Why should I bother to boil bones when I'm loaded with gold?'

Peter 'I can imagine how long your gold will last you! But to keep you from meddling in forbidden ways again, I'll grant you the power to wish anything you please into your knapsack. Now goodbye to you. You will not see me again.'

Scamp 'Goodbye . . . Good riddance more like, you peculiar person. I shan't be running to catch up with you!' And he gave no more thought to the magical power of his knapsack.

Brother Scamp travelled on with his gold, and squandered and wasted it the same as before. When he only had four shillings left, he came to a place where there was a magnificent castle, and not far from it a wretched inn.

53

He went to the inn and asked for a bed for the night, but the inn-keeper refused him, saying:

Inn-Keeper 'There is no room. The house is full of noblemen.'

Scamp 'That's odd. Why would they choose this place instead of that splendid castle?'

Inn-Keeper 'Well, you see, it's not easy to spend a night in that castle. Some have tried, but no one has ever come out alive.'

Scamp 'If others have tried, so will I.'

Inn-Keeper 'Don't even think of it. It will be the end of you. It is possessed by eight ugly devils.'

Scamp 'Don't worry about me. Just give me the keys and something to eat and drink.'

So the man gave him the keys and some food and wine and Brother Scamp went into the castle and enjoyed his meal. After a while, he felt sleepy and lay down on the floor because there was no bed. He soon fell fast asleep.

But in the middle of the night he is awakened by a terrifying noise. When he opens his eyes, he sees eight ugly Devils dancing round him in a circle.

Scamp 'Dance as much as you like, but stay away from me.'

The Devils come closer and closer and nearly step on his face with their feet.

Scamp 'Stop it, you fiends!'

But their frenzy gets worse. Brother Scamp becomes very angry.

Scamp 'Quiet, I said!'

He grabs a table-leg and sets about them with it, but eight Devils are too many for one soldier. While he is hitting the one in front of him, the ones behind him grab his hair and yank fiercely.

Scamp 'Stinking devils! This is too much. But now I'll show you something. All eight of you into my knapsack!'

They disappear into the knapsack. He buckles it, flings it into a corner, and at last everything is still. Brother Scamp lies down again and sleeps until morning.

Scamp The inn-keeper and the nobleman who owned the castle arrived to see what had happened to him. They were astonished to find him alive and well.

Nobleman 'Didn't the ghosts harm you?'

Scamp 'How could they harm me? I've got them all in my knapsack. Now you can live in your castle again. The ghosts won't bother you any more.'

Nobleman The nobleman thanked him, rewarded him generously and begged him to stay in his service and he would provide for him till death.

Scamp 'No, I'm used to wandering about. I'll just get on my way.'

Back on the road, Brother Scamp stopped at a smithy, put the knapsack full of devils on the anvil, and asked the blacksmith and his apprentices to batter it with all their might. The devils screamed dreadfully, and when he opened the knapsack seven were dead; but one, who had been in a crease, was still alive. That one scuttled away and went to Hell.

After this, Brother Scamp travelled about for a long time, and if anyone knows what he got up to, they'll have a long tale to tell. Finally, he grew old and his thoughts turned to death; so he went to a hermit who was respected as a Holy Man and said: 'I'm tired of knocking about, and now I want to see about getting into the Kingdom of Heaven.'

Hermit 'There are two roads. One is broad and pleasant and leads to Hell. The other is narrow and rough and leads to Heaven.'

Scamp 'I'd be daft to take the rough and narrow way.' Sure enough, he took the broad, pleasant way and fetched up at a big black gate.

It was the Gate of Hell. He knocked, and the gate-keeper squinted out to see who was there.

Eighth Devil When he saw Brother Scamp, he nearly leapt out of his skin, for he just happened to be the eighth devil in the knapsack who'd escaped with only a black eye. Fast as a rat, he slammed, locked and bolted the gate, and fled to the Head Devil. 'There's a man outside with a knapsack,' he said. 'He wants to come in, but for Hell's sake don't let him, or he'll wish all Hell into his knapsack. He had me in it once, and what a terrible pounding I got!'

Head Devil Brother Scamp was told he couldn't come in and should clear off.

Scamp 'If they won't give me a welcome here, I'll see if there's room for me in Heaven. I've got to stay somewhere.'

So he turned around and travelled until he came to the Gate of Heaven, and knocked upon it. His old comrade happened to be on duty as gate-keeper, and Brother Scamp recognised him right away as St Peter. 'Well, look who it is!' he thought. 'My old comrade will give me a warmer reception.'

Peter 'I don't believe it! You think you can get into Heaven?'

Scamp 'Let me in, Brother, I've got to go somewhere. They wouldn't take me in Hell, or I wouldn't be standing here now.'

Peter 'Too bad, you're not getting in here.'

Scamp 'Well, if you really won't allow me in then take back your knapsack, because I don't want to keep anything of yours.'

Peter 'Hand it over then.'

Scamp He passed the knapsack through the railings and St Peter hung it up behind his chair.

'Now, I wish myself into the knapsack!'

And whoosh! There he was in the knapsack. The knapsack was in Heaven, and St Peter had to let him stay there. Fair enough.

Note

The following stories were not dramatized in the same fashion as the preceding ones. At each performance, a selection of these stories was simply told by one or more of the actors.

The Fox and the Geese
Travelling
The Golden Key
Two Households
Fair Katrinelje
Knoist and His Three Sons
Sweet Porridge
The Ungrateful Son
The Wise Servant

The order of the stories remained open throughout the run, although the first half would always end with 'The Fox and the Geese' (after 'Snow White') and the second with 'The Golden Key' (after 'Brother Scamp').

For the stories themselves, please refer to the following section of the book.

More Grimm Tales

Adapted by Carol Ann Duffy

Little Red-Cap

There was once a delicious little girl who was loved by everyone who saw her, but most of all by her grandmother who was always wondering what treat to give the sweet child next. Once she sent her a little red cap which suited her so well that she wouldn't wear anything else and she was known from then on as Little Red-Cap.

One day her Mother said, 'Little Red-Cap, here are some cakes and a bottle of best wine. Take them to Grandmother. She's been poorly and is still a bit weak and these will do her good. Now, hurry up before it gets too hot. And mind how you go, like a good little girl. And don't go wandering off the path or you'll fall over and break the wine-bottle – because there will be none left for Grandmother if you do. And when you go into her room, make sure you say "Good morning" nicely, instead of peeping into every corner first!' Little Red-Cap held her mother's hand and said, 'Don't worry, I'll do everything just as you say.'

Her grandmother lived out in the wood, a half-an-hour's walk from the village, and as soon as Little Red-Cap stepped into the wood, a wolf saw her. Because she didn't know what a wicked animal it was, she wasn't afraid of it.

'Good morning, Little Red-Cap,' it said.

'Thank-you, Wolf.'

'And where might you be going so early?'

'To my Grandmother's house.'

'And what's that you're carrying in your apron?'

'Cakes and wine. We were baking yesterday – and my poor grandmother has been ill, so these will strengthen her.'

'Where does Grandmother live, Little Red-Cap?'

'She lives a quarter-of-an-hour's walk from here, under the three big oak trees. Her house has hazel hedges near it. I'm sure you know it.'

But the wolf was thinking to itself, 'How young and sweet and tender she is. I could eat her. She'll make a plumper mouthful for my jaws than the old woman. If I am wily, though, I can have the pair of them!' So it walked beside Little Red-Cap for a bit, and then said, 'Look, Little Red-Cap. Open your eyes and see! There are beautiful flowers all around us. And there's wonderful birdsong that you don't even listen to. You just plod straight ahead as though you were going to school – and yet the woods are such fun!'

So Little Red-Cap looked around her and when she saw the sunbeams seeming to wink at her among the trees, and when she saw the tempting flowers leading away from the straight path, she thought, 'Grandmother will be very pleased if I pick her a bunch of lovely fresh flowers. And it's still early, so I've got plenty of time.' So she ran from the path, among the trees, picking her flowers, and she kept seeing prettier and prettier flowers which led her deeper and deeper into the wood.

But the bad wolf ran fast and straight to the Grand-mother's house and knocked on the door. 'Who's there?' called out Grandmother.

'Only Little Red-Cap bringing you cake and wine. Open the door.'

'Lift the latch. I'm too feeble to get up.'

So the wolf lifted the latch and the door flew open and without even a word it leapt on the old woman's bed and gobbled her up. Then it pulled her clothes and her night-cap over its wolfy fur, crawled into her bed and closed the curtains.

All this time, Little Red-Cap had been trotting about among the flowers and when she'd picked as many as her arms could hold, she remembered her Grandmother and hurried off to her house. She was surprised to see that the door was open and as soon as she stepped inside she felt very strange and said to herself, 'Oh dear, I always look forward to seeing Grandmother, so why do I feel so nervous today?'

'Good Morning?' she said, but there was no reply. So she walked over to the bed and drew back the curtains.

Grandmother lay there with her nightcap pulled right down over her face, looking very peculiar indeed.

'Oh, Grandmother, what big ears you have!'

'The better to hear you with, my sweet.'

'Oh, Grandmother, what big eyes you have!'

'The better to see you with, my love.'

'Oh, Grandmother, what big hands you have!'

'The better to touch you with.'

'But Grandmother, what a terrible big mouth you have.'

'The better to eat you.'

And as soon as the words had left its drooling lips, the wolf made one leap from the bed and gobbled up poor Little Red-Cap. When it had had its fill, the wolf dragged itself onto the bed, fell fast asleep and started to snore very loudly. The Huntsman was just passing the house and thought, 'How loudly the old woman is snoring. I'd better see if something is wrong.' So he went into the house and when he reached the bed he saw the wolf spread out in it.

'So you've come here, you old sinner. I've wanted to catch you for a long, long time.' The Huntsman took aim with his gun and was about to shoot when it flashed through his mind that the wolf might have swallowed the Grandmother whole and that she might still be saved. So instead of firing, he got a good pair of scissors and began to snip the belly of the sleeping wolf.

After two snips he saw the bright red colour of the little red cap. Two snips, three snips, four snips more and out jumped Little Red-Cap, crying, 'Oh, how frightened I've been! It's so dark inside the wolf!' And then out came the Grandmother, hardly breathing, but still alive. Little Red-Cap rushed outside and quickly fetched some big stones and they filled the wolf's belly with them. When the wolf woke up, it tried to run away, but the great stones in its evil gut were too heavy and it dropped down dead.

When this happened, all three were delighted. The Huntsman skinned the wolf and went home with its pelt. The Grandmother ate the cake and drank the wine and soon began to feel much better. And Little Red-Cap promised herself, 'Never so long as I live will I wander off the path into the woods when my mother has warned me not to.'

'Where are you going?'

'To Walpe.'

'You to Walpe, me to Walpe, so, so, together we'll go.'

'Got a man? What's his name?'

'Dan.'

'Your man Dan, my man Dan, you to Walpe, me to Walpe, so, so, together we'll go.'

'Got a child? How's he styled?'

'Wild.'

'Your child Wild, my child Wild, your man Dan, my man Dan, you to Walpe, me to Walpe, so, so, together we'll go.'

'Got a cradle? What's its label?'

'Hippodadle.'

'Your cradle Hippodadle, my cradle Hippodadle, your child Wild, my child Wild, your man Dan, my man Dan, you to Walpe, me to Walpe, so, so, together we'll go.'

'Got a servant? What's his title?'

'Stay-a-Bed Bone-Idle.'

'Your Servant Stay-a-Bed Bone-Idle, my Servant, Stay-a-Bed Bone-Idle, your cradle Hippodadle, my cradle Hippodadle, your child Wild, my child Wild, your man Dan, my man Dan, you to Walpe, me to Walpe, so, so, together we'll go.'

The Fox and the Geese

One day the fox came to a meadow and there sat a flock of fine geese. The fox smiled and said, 'My timing is perfect. There you are all sitting together quite beautifully, so that I can eat you up one after the other.' The geese cackled with terror, jumped up and began to wail and plead piteously for their lives. But the fox would have none of it and said, 'Begging is useless. There is no mercy to be had. You must die.'

At last, one of the geese stepped up and said, 'If we poor geese are to lose our healthy young lives, then please allow us one last prayer so that we do not die with our sins on our conscience. One final prayer and then we will line up in a row so that you can always pick the plumpest first.'

The fox thought, 'Yes, that's a reasonable request, and a pious one too.'

'Pray away, geese. I'll wait till you are finished.'

So the first goose began a good long prayer, for ever saying 'Ga! Ga!' and, as she wouldn't stop, the second didn't wait her turn but started praying away also. 'Ga! Ga!' The third and the fourth followed her – 'Ga! Ga!' – and soon they were all praying and honking and cackling together.

When they have finished praying, this story shall be continued further, but at the moment they are still very busy praying. Ga! Ga!

Clever Hans

Hans's mother said, 'Where are you off to Hans?' Hans said, 'To see Gretel.' 'Behave well, Hans.' 'Oh, I'll behave well. Goodbye Mother.' 'Goodbye, Hans.'

Hans goes to Gretel. 'Good day, Gretel.' 'Good day, Hans. What have you brought that's good?' 'I've brought nowt. I want to have something given me.' Gretel presents Hans with a needle. 'Goodbye, Gretel.' 'Goodbye, Hans.'

Hans takes the needle, sticks it into a hay cart, follows the cart home. 'Good evening, mother.' 'Good evening, Hans. Where have you been?' 'With Gretel.' 'What did Gretel give you?' 'Gave me a needle.' 'Where is the needle, Hans?' 'Stuck in the hay cart.' 'That was poorly done, Hans. You should have stuck the needle in your sleeve.' 'Not to worry. I'll do better next time.'

'Where are you off to, Hans? 'To Gretel, Mother.' 'Behave well, Hans.' 'Oh, I'll behave well. Goodbye, Mother.' 'Goodbye, Hans.'

Hans takes the needle, sticks it into a hay-cart, follows the cart home. 'Good evening, mother.' 'Good evening, Hans. Where have you been?' 'With Gretel.' 'What did you take her?' 'Took nowt. Got something given.' What did Gretel give you?' 'Gave me a needle.' 'Where is the needle, Hans?' 'Stuck in the hay-cart.' 'That was poorly done, Hans. You should have stuck the needle in your sleeve.' 'Not to worry. I'll do better next time.'

'Where are you off to, Hans?' 'To Gretel's, Mother.' 'Behave well, Hans.' 'Oh, I'll behave well. Goodbye, Mother.' 'Goodbye, Hans.'

Hans goes to Gretel. 'Good day, Gretel.' 'Good day, Hans. What have you brought that's good?' 'I've brought nowt. I want to have something given to me.' Gretel presents Hans with a knife. 'Goodbye, Gretel.' 'Goodbye, Hans.'

Hans takes the knife, sticks it in his sleeve, and goes home. 'Good evening, Mother.' 'Good evening, Hans. Where have you been?' 'With Gretel.' 'What did you take her?' 'Took nowt. Got given something.' 'What did Gretel give you?' 'Gave me a knife.' 'Where is the knife, Hans?' 'Stuck in my sleeve.' 'That was poorly done, Hans. You should have put the knife in your pocket.' 'Not to worry. Do better next time.'

'Where are you off to, Hans?' 'To Gretel, Mother.' 'Behave well, Hans.' 'Oh, I'll behave well. Goodbye, Mother.' 'Goodbye, Hans.'

Hans goes to Gretel. 'Good day, Gretel.' 'Good day, Hans. What good thing have you brought?' 'I've brought nowt. I want something given me.' Gretel presents Hans with a young goat.

Hans takes the goat, ties its legs and puts it in his pocket. When he gets home it has suffocated. 'Good evening, Mother.' 'Good evening, Hans. Where have you been?' 'With Gretel.' 'What did you take her?' 'Took nowt. Got given something.' 'What did Gretel give you?' 'She gave me a goat.' 'Where is the goat, Hans?' 'Put it in my pocket.' 'That was poorly done, Hans. You should have put a rope round the goat's neck.' 'Not to worry. Do better next time.'

'Where are you off to, Hans?' 'To Gretel, Mother.' 'Behave well, Hans.' 'Oh. I'll behave well. Goodbye, Mother.' 'Goodbye, Hans.'

Hans goes to Gretel. 'Good day, Gretel.' 'Good day, Hans. What good thing have you brought?' 'I've brought nowt. I want something given me.' Gretel presents Hans with a piece of bacon. 'Goodbye, Gretel.' 'Goodbye, Hans.'

Hans takes the bacon, ties it to a rope and drags it away behind him. The dogs come sniffing and scoff the bacon.

When he gets home he has the rope in his hand with nothing at the end of it. 'Good evening, Mother.' 'Good evening, Hans. Where have you been?' 'With Gretel.' 'What did you take her?' 'Took nowt. Got given something.' 'What did Gretel give you?' 'Gave me a bit of bacon.' 'Where is the bacon, Hans?' 'I tied it to a rope, pulled it home. Dogs had it.' 'That was poorly done, Hans. You should have carried the bacon on your head.' 'Not to worry. Do better next time.'

'Where are you off to Hans?' 'To Gretel, Mother.' 'Behave well, Hans.' 'Oh, I'll behave well. Good bye, Mother.' 'Good bye, Hans.'

Hans goes to Gretel. 'Good day, Gretel.' 'Good day, Hans. What have you brought me that's good?' 'I've brought nowt. I want something given me.' Gretel presents Hans with a calf. 'Good bye, Gretel.' 'Good bye, Hans.'

Hans takes the calf and puts it on his head. The calf gives his face a kicking. 'Good evening, Mother.' 'Good evening, Hans. Where have you been?' 'With Gretel.' 'What did you take her?' 'Took nowt. Got given something.' 'What did Gretel give you?' 'A calf.' 'Where is the calf, Hans?' 'I put it on my head and it kicked my face.' 'That was poorly done, Hans. You should have led the calf and put it in the stable.' 'Not to worry. Do better next time.'

'Where are you off to, Hans?' 'To Gretel, Mother.' 'Behave well, Hans.' 'Oh, I'll behave well. Good bye, Mother.' 'Good bye, Hans.'

Hans goes to Gretel. 'Good day, Gretel.' 'Good day, Hans. What good thing have you brought?' 'I've brought nowt. I want something given me.' Gretel says to Hans, 'I will come with you.'

Hans takes Gretel, ties her to a rope, leads her to the stable and binds her tight. Then Hans goes to his mother. 'Good evening, Mother.' 'Good evening, Hans. Where have you been?' 'With Gretel.' 'What did you take her?' 'I took her nowt.' 'What did Gretel give you?' 'She gave me nowt. She came back with me.' 'Where have you left Gretel?' 'I led her by the rope, tied her up in the stable, and scattered a bit of grass for her.' 'That was poorly done, Hans. You should have cast warm eyes on her.' 'Not to worry. Will do better.'

Hans marched into the stable, cut out all the calves' and sheep's eyes, and threw them in Gretel's face. Then Gretel became very angry, tore herself loose and ran away. Gretel was no longer the bride of Hans.

Knoist and His Three Sons

Somewhere between Werrel and Soist lived a man whose name was Knoist and he had three sons. One was blind, the other was lame and the third was stark bollock-naked. Once upon a time, they went into a field and there they saw a hare. The blind one shot it, the lame one caught it and the naked one put it in his pocket. Then they came to a mighty great lake, upon which three boats bobbed.

One sailed, the other sank, and the third had no bottom. All three lads got into the one with no bottom. Then they came to a mighty great forest in the middle of which was a mighty great tree in the middle of which was a mighty great church. Inside the church was a sexton made of beech-wood and a parson made of box-wood, and the pair of them dealt out holy water with cudgels.

> 'He'll be happy if he's the one
> 'Who can from Holy Water run.'

Sweet Porridge

for Ella

Once upon a different time there was a very good little girl who lived with her Mother; but they were so poor they had nothing left to eat. So the little girl went into the forest. An old woman met her, who knew of her troubles. She gave her a small pot which when she said, 'Cook, little pot, cook!' would cook sweet and nourishing porridge. When she said 'Stop, little pot,' it would stop cooking.

The girl took the pot home to her Mother and from then on they were no longer hungry and ate good sweet porridge whenever they wanted.

One day, when the little girl had gone out, her Mother said, 'Cook, little pot, cook.' And it cooked away and she ate till she was quite full up. She wanted the pot to stop cooking then, but she didn't know the words. So it carried on cooking, cooking, until the porridge spilled over the brim; and it carried on cooking, cooking, until the kitchen was full, then the whole house, then the house next door, then the whole street; and it carried on cooking, cooking, as though it wanted to satisfy the hunger of the whole world. It caused the greatest inconvenience and distress, but no one knew how to stop it.

At last, when there was only one single house left, like one spud on a plate, the little girl came home and said: 'Stop, little pot!' And it stopped and gave up cooking. But anyone who wanted to return to the town had to eat their way back in.

The Hare and the Hedgehog

This tale, my splendid young listeners, may seem to you to be false, but it really is true, because I heard it from my grandfather, and when he told it he always said, 'It must be true, my dear, or else no one could tell it to you.' This is the story.

One Sunday morning around harvest time, just as the buckwheat was blooming, the sun was shining, the breeze was blowing, the larks were singing, the bees were buzzing, the folk were off to church in their Sunday best, everything that lived was happy and the hedgehog was happy too.

The hedgehog was stood by his own front door, arms akimbo, relishing the morning and singing a song to himself half-aloud. It was no better or worse a song than the songs which hedgehogs usually sing on a Sabbath morning. His wife was inside, washing and drying the children, and he suddenly decided that he'd take a stroll in the field and see how his turnips were doing. The turnips grew beside the hedgehog's house and the hedgehog family were accustomed to eating them – because of this he thought of them as his own. The hedgehog clicked shut his front door and set off for the field. He hadn't gone very far, and was just turning round the sloe-bush which grows outside the field, to go up into the turnip-field, when he noticed the hare. The hare was out and about on a similar errand to visit his cabbages. The hedgehog called out a friendly good morning. But the hare, a distinguished gentleman in his own way, was hoity-toity and gave the hedgehog a snooty look. He didn't say good morning back, but spoke in a very contemptuous manner:

'What brings you scampering about in the field so early in the morning?'

'I'm taking a walk,' said the hedgehog.

'A walk!' said the hare with a haughty sneer. 'Surely you can think of a better use for those legs of yours.'

These words made the hedgehog livid with rage, for he couldn't bear any reference to his legs, which are naturally crooked.

The hedgehog said, 'You seem to think you can do more with your legs than I can with mine.'

'That's exactly what I think.'

'That can soon be put to the test. I'll wager that if we run a race, I shall beat you.'

'That's preposterous! With those hedgehoggy legs! Well, I'm perfectly willing if you have such an absurd fancy for it. What shall we wager?'

'A golden sovereign and a bottle of brandy.'

'Done. Shake hands on it. We might as well do it at once.'

But the hedgehog said, 'Nay, nay, there's no rush. I'm going home for some breakfast. I'll be back at this spot in half-an-hour.'

The hare was quite satisfied with this, so the hedgehog set off home. On his way he thought to himself, 'The hare is betting on his long legs, but I'll get the better of him. He may be an important gentleman, but he's a foolish fellow and he'll pay for what he's said.'

When the hedgehog got back home, he called to his wife: 'Wife, dress yourself quickly. You've got to come up to the field with me.'

'What's going on?' said his wife. 'I've made a wager with the hare for a gold sovereign and a bottle of brandy, and we have to race each other. You must be there.'

But his wife was aghast. 'Husband, are you not right in the head? Have you completely lost your wits? What are you thinking of, running a race with the hare?'

The hedgehog snapped, 'Hold your tongue, woman, that's my affair. Don't try to discuss things which are matters for men. Now get yourself dressed and come with me.'

What else was the wife of a hedgehog to do? She had to obey him, like it or like it not.

So they set off together and the hedgehog told his wife. 'Pay attention to what I'm saying. The long field will be our race-course. I'll run in one furrow and the hare in the other. We'll start from the top. You position yourself at the bottom of the furrow. When the hare arrives at the end of the furrow next to you, just shout out 'I'm here already.'

They reached the field. The hedgehog showed his wife her place, then walked up top to meet the hare.

'Shall we start then?' said the hare.

'Ready when you are,' said the hedgehog.

'Then both at once.'

They each got in their furrow. The hare counted 'Once. Twice. Thrice and Away!' and flew off at the speed of arrogance down the field. But the hedgehog only ran three steps, then crouched down, quiet and sleekit in his furrow.

As soon as the hare the arrived full pelt at the bottom of field, the hedgehog's wife was already there saying, 'I'm here already.' The hare was flabbergasted. He thought it really was the hedgehog because the wife looked just like her husband. But he thought. 'This hasn't been done fairly.' He said, 'We must run again. Let us do it again.' And a second time he whooshed off like a whirlwind. But the hedgehog's wife stayed modestly in her place and when the hare reached the other end of the field, there was the hedgehog himself crying out, 'I'm here already!' The hare was hopping with fury, and kept saying, 'Again! Again! We must run it again!' The hedgehog said, 'Fine. I'm happy to run as often as you choose.'

The hare ran another seventy-three times. Each time, the hedgehog tricked him. Every time the hare reached one

75

end of the field, the hedgehog or his wife said, 'I'm here already.' But at the seventy-fourth time, the hare couldn't make it to the end. He collapsed in the middle of the field and a ribbon of blood streamed from his mouth. The hare was dead. The hedgehog ran up and took the gold sovereign which he had won and the bottle of brandy. He called his wife out of the furrow and the pair of them strolled home on their eight legs in great delight. If they're not dead, they're still living there.

The moral of this story is, firstly, that no matter how grand a person might be, they should not poke fun at anyone beneath themselves – not even a hedgehog. Secondly, it shows that a man should marry someone in his own position, who looks just like he looks himself. Whoever is a hedgehog must make quite sure that his wife is a hedgehog as well. And so on. And so forth.

Travelling

A poor woman had a son and the son longed to travel. But his mother said, 'How can you go travelling? We have no money for you to take with you.'

Then the son said, 'I will manage very well for myself. I will always say "Not much, not much".' So he walked for a long time and always said, 'Not much, not much, not much.' Then he passed by a group of fishermen and said, 'Good luck to you. Not much, not much, not much.'

And when the net was hauled in, they hadn't caught much fish. So one of them grabbed the youth and waved his stick and said, 'Have you seen me threshing?'

'What should I have said, then?' asked the youth.

'You must say "Lots more, lots more".'

After this, he walked on for a long time, saying, 'Lots wore, lots more', until he came to the gallows where they were about to hang a poor sinner. He called out, 'Good morning. Lots more, lots more.'

'What did you say, scoundrel, lots more? Do you want to make out there are more wicked people to hang? Isn't this enough?' He got some more thwacks on his back.

'What should I have said?'

'You must say "God have mercy on the poor soul".'

So, once more, the youth walked for a long time saying, 'God have mercy on the poor soul.' He came to a pit where a knacker was chopping up a dead horse. The youth said, 'Good morning. God have mercy on the poor soul.'

'What did you say, you cheeky good-for-nothing?' The knacker gave him such a clout on the ear that he saw stars.

'What should I say, then?'

'You must say, "Into the pit it must go".'

He walked on again, saying, 'Into the pit it must go, into the pit it must go.' He came to a cart full of people. He said, 'Good morning, into the pit it must go.' Then the cart and everyone in it fell into a pit and the driver grabbed his whip and cracked it over the youth's back. He was forced to crawl home to his mother, and as long as he lived he never went travelling again.

Snow White

In the cold heart of winter, when snow fell as though the white sky had been torn into a million pieces, a Queen sat by a window sewing. The frame of the window was made of black ebony. And while the Queen was sewing and looking out at the snow, she pricked her finger with the needle and three drops of blood fell upon the snow. The red looked so pretty against the white that the Queen suddenly thought to herself, 'I wish I had a child as white as snow, as red as blood and as black as the wood on the window-frame.'

Soon after that, she had a little daughter who was as white as snow, with lips as red as blood and hair as black as ebony. She was called Snow White and when she was born, the Queen died.

After a year had gone by, the King married again. His new wife was a beautiful woman, but she was proud and vain and couldn't bear the thought of anyone else being more beautiful. She owned a wonderful mirror and when she stood before it, looking at her reflection, and said:

> 'Mirror, mirror on the wall,
> Who in this land is fairest of all?'

the mirror replied:

> 'You are, Queen. Fairest of all.'

Then she was pleased because she knew the mirror always told the truth.

But Snow White was growing up, and becoming more and more beautiful. And when she was seven years old she was as lovely as the day and ever, and more beautiful than the Queen herself. One day, the Queen asked her mirror:

> 'Mirror, mirror on the wall,
> Who in this land is fairest of all?'

And the mirror answered:

> 'Queen, you are beautiful, day and night,
> But even more lovely is little Snow White.'

Then the Queen got a shock, and turned yellow and green with poisonous envy. From that moment, whenever she looked at Snow White, her heart turned sour in her breast, she hated her so much. Envy and pride crept and coiled round her heart like ugly weeds, so that she could get no peace night or day. At last she called a huntsman and said, 'Take the girl into the forest. I want her out of my sight. Kill her – and fetch me back her lungs and liver to prove it.'

The huntsman did what she said and took Snow White away – but when he pulled out his knife to stab her innocent heart, Snow White cried and said, 'Please dear huntsman, spare my life! I will run away into the wild woods and never come back.'

And as she was so beautiful, the huntsman took pity on her and said, 'Poor child. Run away then.' 'The wild beasts will eat you soon enough,' he thought, but he felt as though a cruel hand had stopped squeezing his heart because he wasn't going to kill her. A young boar ran by and he slaughtered it, cut out its lungs and liver and took them to the Queen to prove the girl was dead. The cook had to salt them and the bad Queen ate them up and thought she'd eaten Snow White's lungs and liver.

But Snow White was alone in the forest and terrified. She began to run, over stones as sharp as envy, through thorns as cruel as long fingernails. Wild beasts ran past her but did her no harm. She ran as long as her feet could carry her, until it was almost evening. It was then that she saw a little cottage and went into it to rest. Everything in the cottage was small, but neater and cleaner than can be told. There was a table with a white table-cloth and seven little plates, each with a little spoon. There were seven little knives and forks and seven little tankards. Against the wall were seven little beds side by side, each one covered with a snow-white eiderdown.

Snow White was so hungry and thirsty that she ate a morsel of bread and vegetables from each plate and sipped a swallow of wine from each mug. She was so sleepy that she lay down on one of the little beds, but none of them suited her. One was too long, one too short, one too soft, one too hard, one too lumpy, one too smooth. But the seventh was just right, so she snuggled down in it, said a prayer, and went to sleep.

When it was dark, the owners of the cottage came back. They were seven dwarfs who worked in the mountains digging for gold and copper. They lit their seven candles to fill the cottage with light and at once saw that someone had been there.

The first said: 'Who's been sitting in my chair?'
The second: 'Who's been eating off my plate?'
The third: 'Who's had some of my bread?'
The fourth: 'Who's been biting my vegetables?'
The fifth: 'Who's been using my fork?'
The sixth: 'Who's been cutting with my knife?'

Then the first one looked about and saw there was a little hollow on his bed, and he said, "Who's been lying on my bed?' The others crowded round and each one shouted out 'Somebody's been getting into my bed too!' But the seventh one found Snow White lying asleep in his bed, and he called the others. They cried out with amazement and fetched their seven little candles and let the light fall on Snow White. 'Oh goodness! Oh mercy!' they said, 'What a beautiful child.'

They were so pleased that they let her sleep peacefully on. The seventh dwarf slept with his companions, one hour with each, and so passed the night, and was glad to do so.

When morning came, Snow White awoke and was frightened when she saw the seven dwarfs. But they were friendly and asked her her name. 'My name is Snow White,' she replied. 'How have you come to our house?' asked the dwarfs. She told them that her step-mother had ordered her to be killed, but that the huntsman had taken pity on her and she had run through the forest for a whole day until she arrived at their little cottage.

The dwarf said: 'If you will take care of our house, make the beds, set the table, keep everything neat and tidy, cook, wash, sew, knit and mend, you can stay here with us and you shall want for nothing.'

'With all my heart!' said Snow White, and she stayed with the seven dwarfs. She kept the house exactly as they wanted. In the mornings they went off to the mountain to dig and delve for copper and gold. In the evenings they returned and then their supper had to be ready. The young girl was alone all day, so the dwarfs warned her to be careful. 'Beware of your step-mother. She will soon find out you are here. Don't let anyone into the house.'

But the Queen believed that she'd eaten the lungs Snow White breathed with, and that once again she was more beautiful than anyone. She went to her mirror and said:

> 'Mirror, mirror, on the wall
> Who in this land is fairest of all?'

And the mirror replied:

> 'Queen, you're the fairest I can see.
> But deep in the wood where seven dwarfs dwell,
> Snow White is still alive and well
> And you are not so fair as she.'

Then the Queen was appalled because she knew that the mirror never lied and that the huntsman had tricked her. Her envious heart gnawed away inside her and her wicked mind thought and thought how she might kill Snow White – for so long as she wasn't the fairest in the land she could have no peace.

When at last she had thought of a plan, she stained her face and dressed-up like an old pedlar-woman, so that not even her own mirror would have known her. In this disguise she made her way to the house of the seven dwarfs. She knocked at the door and sang out: 'Pretty things for sale, very cheap, very cheap.'

Snow White looked out of the window and called back: 'Good day, pedlar-woman, what are you selling today?'

'Beautiful things, pretty things, fair things, skirt-laces of all colours.'

The sly Queen pulled out a lace of bright-coloured silk. 'I can let this friendly old woman in,' thought Snow White, and she unlocked the door and bought the fine laces.

But the old woman said, 'Child, what a sight you are! Come here and let the old pedlar-woman lace you properly for once.' Snow White wasn't suspicious at all and stood before her and let herself be laced with the new laces. But the old woman laced so quickly and viciously and tightly that Snow White lost her breath and fell down as if she were dead. 'Now I am the most beautiful,' crowed the Queen and hurried away.

Soon afterwards, when evening fell, the seven dwarfs came home – but how distressed they were to see their dear little Snow White lying on the ground. They lifted her up and, when they saw she was laced too tightly, they cut the laces. Then Snow White started to breathe a little and after a while came back to life. When the dwarfs heard what had happened, they said, 'The old pedlar-woman was no one else but the evil Queen. Be careful. Let nobody in when we are not with you.'

The Queen ran home and went straight to her mirror:

'Mirror, mirror, on the wall
Who in this land is fairest of all?'

And the mirror replied as before:

'Deep in the wood where seven dwarfs dwell,
Snow White is still alive and well.
Although you're the fairest I can see,
Queen, you are not so fair as she.'

When she heard the mirror's words, the Queen's blood flooded her heart with fear, for she knew it was true that Snow White was alive.

But she said, 'Now I will think of something that will really rid me of you for ever.' And by the help of witchcraft, which she understood, she made a poisonous comb. Then she disguised herself in the shape of another old woman, made her malevolent way to the house of the seven dwarfs and knocked at the door.

'Good things for sale, cheap, cheap.'

Snow White looked out and said, 'Go away please. I can't let anyone in.

'You can at least look,' said the old woman, and held out the poisonous comb.

Snow White admired the comb so much that she let herself be fooled and opened the door. When they had agreed a price, the old woman said, 'Now I'll comb your ebony hair properly for once.'

Poor Snow White had no suspicion and let the old woman do as she wished. But no sooner had the crone put the comb in the girl's hair than the poison took effect and Snow White fell down senseless.

'You prize beauty,' spat the wicked woman, 'You are nothing now.' And she went away.

As luck would have it, it was nearly evening, when the seven dwarfs were due home. When they saw Snow White

84

left for dead on the ground they at once suspected the step-mother, and they looked and found the poisonous comb. They took it out and Snow White soon came to herself and told them what had happened. Then they warned her once more to be on her guard and to open the door to no one.

The Queen was at home with her mirror:

> 'Mirror, mirror, on the wall,
> Who in this land is fairest of all?'

The mirror answered as before:

> 'Queen, you're the fairest I can see.
> But deep in the woods where seven dwarfs dwell
> Snow White is still alive and well
> And no one's as beautiful as she.'

When she heard the mirror speak like this, the Queen trembled and shook with rage and swore, 'Snow White shall die, even if it costs me my life.'

She went into a quiet, secret, lonely room where no one ever came, and there she made a very poisonous apple. On the outside it looked pretty – crisp and white with a blood-red cheek, so that everyone who saw it longed for it – but whoever ate a piece of it would die.

Then she painted her face, disguised herself as a farmer's wife, and went for the third time to the house of the seven dwarfs. She knocked at the door. Snow White put her head out of the window and said, 'I can't let anyone in. The seven dwarfs have forbidden me.'

'It's all the same to me, dear. I'll soon get rid of my apples. Here – you can have one.'

'No, I dare not take anything.'

'Are you afraid it might be poisoned? Look, I'll cut the apple in two pieces, you eat the red cheek and I will eat the white.' But the apple was so cunningly made that only the red cheek was poisoned. Snow White longed for the tantalising fruit and when she saw the farmer's wife sink her teeth into it, she couldn't resist any more and stretched out her hand and took the poisonous half. But as soon as she'd taken a bite into her mouth, she fell down dead. The Queen gazed at her long and hard with a dreadful look and laughed horribly and said:

> 'Snow White,
> Blood Red,
> Black as Coffin Wood –
> This time the seven dwarfs
> Will find you dead for good.'

She went home quickly. She rushed to her mirror. She asked it again:

> 'Mirror, mirror on the wall,
> Who in this land is fairest of all?'

And the mirror answered at last:

> 'Oh, Queen, in this land you are fairest of all.'

When the dwarfs came home in the evening, they found Snow White lying on the ground. She breathed no longer and was dead. They lifted her up and looked for anything poisonous, unlaced her, combed her hair, washed her in water and wine, but it was all useless. The girl was dead and stayed dead. So they laid her upon a bier and the seven of them sat round it and for three whole days they wept for Snow White.

Then they were going to bury her, but she still looked so alive with her pretty red cheeks. They said, 'We cannot put her in the cold, dark earth.' So they had a coffin of glass made, so that she could be seen from all sides. They laid her in it and put her name on it in gold letters and that she was daughter of a King. They placed the coffin up on the mountain and one of them always guarded it. Birds came, too, to weep for Snow White. First an owl, then a raven and last a dove.

And now Snow White lay for a very long time in her glass coffin as though she were only sleeping; still as white as snow, as red as blood, and with hair as black as ebony.

It happened, though, that a King's son came to the forest and went to the dwarfs' house to spend the night. He saw the coffin glinting like a mirror on the mountain, and he saw Snow White inside it and read what was written there in letters of gold. He said to the dwarfs, 'Let me have the coffin. I will give you anything you name for it.' But the dwarfs answered that they wouldn't part with it for all the treasure in the world. Then he said, 'Let me have it as a gift. My heart cannot beat without seeing Snow White. I will honour and cherish her above all else in this world.' Because he spoke like this, the dwarfs pitied him and gave him the coffin.

The King's son had it carried away on his servants' shoulders. As they did this, they tripped over some tree-roots, and with the jolt the piece of poisonous apple which Snow White had swallowed came out of her throat. Before long, she opened her eyes, lifted the coffin lid and sat up, as warm and alive as love. 'Heavens, where am I?' she asked.

The king's son was shining like an apple with delight and said, 'You are with me.' He told her what had happened and said 'I love you more than my heart can hold. Come with me to my father's palace. Be my wife.'

Snow White was willing and did go with him, and their wedding was held with great show and splendour. Snow White's wicked stepmother was bidden to the feast. When she was dressed in her best jewels and finery, she danced to her mirror and queried:

> 'Mirror, mirror, on the wall
> Who in this land is fairest of all?'

The mirror answered:

'You are the old Queen. That much is true.
But the new young Queen is fairer than you.'

Then the wicked woman cursed and swore and was so demented, so wretched, so distraught, that she could hardly think. At first, she wouldn't go to the feast, but she had no peace, and had to see the young Queen. So she went. And when she walked in she saw that it was Snow White and was unable to move with fear and rage. She stood like a statue of hate. But iron dancing shoes were already heating in the fire. They were brought in with tongs and set before her. Then she was forced to put on the red-hot shoes and she was made to dance, dance, until she dropped down dead.

The Ungrateful Son

Once upon a time, a man and his wife were sat by their front door and they had before them a roasted chicken which they were about to eat together. Just then, the man saw his old father coming and he quickly snatched up the chicken and hid it. The old man came, was given a drink of water, then went away. As soon as he was gone, the son went to fetch the chicken for the table. But when he picked it up, it had turned into a great toad which jumped into his face and squatted there and never went away. If anyone tried to take it off, it spat poisonously and looked as though it would spring in their face – so in the end no one dared to touch it. The ungrateful son was forced to feed the toad every single day or else it fed itself on his face. And thus he went from place to place and had no rest anywhere in this world.

The Wise Servant

How fortunate the master is, and how smoothly every-thing runs in his house, when he has a wise servant who listens to his orders carefully but doesn't carry them out, choosing instead to trust to his own ideas. Clever Hans was a type like this and was once sent out by his master to find a lost cow. He was gone for a very long time, and the master thought: 'Good old Hans doesn't do things by halves.' But when he didn't come back at all, the master was worried that something bad might have happened to him. He set out himself to look for him.

He had to look for ages, but at last he caught sight of the lad running up and down a large field. 'There you are, Hans,' he said when he caught up with him. 'Have you found the cow which I sent you to fetch?'

Hans answered, 'No, Master, I've not found the cow. But neither have I been looking for it.'

'Then what have you been looking for, Hans?'

'Something much better, and that luckily I have found!'

'What is that, Hans?'

'Three blackbirds,' answered Hans.

'And where are they?'

'I can see one of them, I can hear the other, and I'm running after the third,' said Wise Hans.

Let this be a lesson for you. Don't bother yourself with your masters or their orders. Just do whatever comes into your head, whatever you please, and then you'll be acting just as wisely as Clever Hans.

The Musicians of Bremen

A man had a donkey who had worked hard for years carrying heavy sacks of corn to the mill. But the donkey's strength had gone and he was getting more and more unfit for the job. The man was thinking how he could get shut of him and save the expense of feeding him. But the donkey got wind of this and ran away. He set off towards Bremen and thought he might try his luck at being a town-musician. After a while on the road, he came across a hound lying by the roadside, panting away as though he'd run very hard. So the donkey said, 'Hello, old Hound-Dog, what are you gasping like that for?'

The dog answered him, 'Ah, I'm not getting any younger and get weaker every day so I can't hunt any more. My master was going to kill me, so I ran away. But how shall I make my living now?' The donkey said, I'll tell you what. I'm on my way to Bremen to become a town-musician. Why don't you come with me? I'll play the lute and you can play away at the kettle-drum!'

The hound was pleased with this idea and on they went.

Before long, they found a cat slumped by the roadside with a face like three wet Wednesdays.

'Now then, old Lick-Whiskers, what makes you look so miserable?'

The cat answered him: 'How else should I look with my problems? Just because I'm getting on and my teeth are worn to stumps and I prefer to sit dreaming by the fire rather than run about after mice, my mistress wants to drown me. So I've run away. But now, who's to tell me what to do and where to go?'

'Come with us to Bremen to be a town-musician. You're well-known for your caterwauling music of the night!'

The cat was impressed with this plan and on the three of them went.

Quite soon our three runaways came to a farm and there on the gate perched a cockerel crowing like mad. The donkey called out, 'That terrible crowing's going right through us. What on earth's up?'

The cock explained: 'I'm forecasting fine weather, because today's wash-day in Heaven and Our Lady wants to dry Baby Jesus's tiny shirts. But they've got guests coming here for dinner tomorrow, and that callous, hard-hearted housekeeper has told cook to cook me. I've to have my head chopped off tonight, so I'm having a good crow while I can.'

'Preposterous, Redcomb! Come instead with us to Bremen. You'll be better off there than in a casserole. With that voice of yours and our rhythm, we're going to make music the like of which has never been heard!'

The cock thought this seemed an excellent plan and all four of them went on their way together.

Bremen town was too far to reach in a day, though, and in the evening they reached a forest where they decided to spend the night. The donkey and the dog lay down under a large tree, the cat settled herself in the branches, and the cock flew right to the top and perched there. Before he went to sleep, he looked to north, south, east and west and thought he spied a quaver of light in the distance. So he called down to his fellow-musicians that there must be a house nearby for him to see a light. The donkey said, 'Then let's go and find it. The accommodation here's appalling.' The hound said that he wouldn't turn up his nose at a plate of bones with some meat on them.

So they set off in the direction of the light, which got bigger and brighter and more attractive, until they came to a well-lit house, where a band of robbers lived. The donkey, who was the biggest, sneaked up to the window and peeped in.

'What can you see, old Greymule?' asked the cock.

'What can I see! Only a table groaning with wonderful things to eat and drink and a band of robbers sat round it filling their boots!'

'Those words are music to my ears! That's the kind of thing we're after,' said the cock.

'Yes, yes! If only we were inside!'

So the four famished fugitives put their furry or feathery heads together to decide how to get rid of the robbers. At last they thought of a plan. Old Greymule was to stand on his hind-legs with his fore-feet on the window; Old Hound-Dog was to jump on the donkey's back; Old Lick-Whiskers was to climb on the back of the dog; and lastly Redcomb was to fly up and perch on the head of the cat, like a hat.

When they'd finally managed all this, the donkey gave a signal, and they launched into their music. The donkey bray-hay-hayed. The cat made mew-mew-music. The hound went Wopbopawoofwoofbowwowwow. And the cock gave a great big Doody doodle Do. For an encore, they all crashed into the room through the window, smashing the glass and still singing. At this horrifying din, the robbers jumped up and thought that a Banshee had come screaming into the house. The robbers were so terrified for their lives that they fled freaked into the forest. At this our four friends sat down at the table, well pleased with what was left, and feasted as though they wouldn't see food and drink for a fortnight.

When our four musicians had finished their meal, they put out the light and found somewhere comfortable to sleep, each according to his needs and nature. The donkey dossed down in the dung-heap in the yard. The hound hunched down behind the door. The cat curled up near the ashes on the hearth. And the cock flapped up to roost in the rafters. They were all so tired after their long journey that they soon fell fast asleep.

The robbers were watching the house from a safe distance. When midnight had passed, and they saw that the light was out and all was quiet, their captain said: 'Well, now. Perhaps we shouldn't have let ourselves be frightened off so easily.' He ordered one of his men to go back to the house and investigate.

The man found everything as silent and dark as a closed piano-lid, as hushed as drowned bagpipes. He fetched a candle from the kitchen. He thought that the burning red eyes of the cat were glowing coals and stuck his match in them to light it. But the cat didn't appreciate the humour of this and flew in his face, scratching and spitting. The man was terrified out of his wits and ran for the back door – but he trod on the dog who leapt up and bit him savagely on the leg. He fled for his life into the yard and was about to leap over the dung-heap when he received a whopping kick in the arse from the donkey. All this commotion had wakened the cock, who began to crow on his perch. 'Cock a doodle do! Cock a doodle do!'

The robber ran as fast as he could back to his mates and said to the Captain: 'Oh, my God! There's a horrible witch in the house. I felt her ratty breath and her long claws on my face. Oh God! There's a man with a knife by the back door who stabbed me in the leg. Oh! There's a black monster in the yard who beat me with a wooden club. God! And to top it all, there's a judge on the roof and he called out, 'That's the crook that'll do! The crook that'll do!' So I got out of there as fast as I could.'

After that, the robbers didn't dare go back to the house. But the four talented members of the Bremen Town Band liked the house so much that they just stayed on. And they're still there.

This story has been told for years. The mouth of the last person to tell this tale still has a warm tongue in it – as you can see.

The Golden Key

It was winter, and deep snow covered the ground, when a poor boy was made to go out on a sledge to fetch wood. When he had gathered enough, and packed it all, he thought that before he went home he would light a fire to warm his frozen limbs. So he scraped away the snow and as he was making a clear space he found a tiny golden key. As soon as he picked it up he thought that where there was a key there must also be a lock. So he dug in the ground and discovered a small iron chest. He thought: 'If the key only fits there are bound to be precious treasures in this little box.' He searched everywhere but couldn't find a keyhole. At last he found one which was so small that it could hardly be seen. He tried the key in the lock and it fitted perfectly. Then he turned the key round once. And now we must wait until he has quite finished unlocking it and then we shall find out what wonderful things were lying in that box.

Rumpelstiltskin

There was a miller once who was very poor but he had one daughter more beautiful than any treasure. It happened one day that he came to speak to the King and to make himself look special he said, 'I have a daughter who can spin straw into gold.' Now this King was very fond of gold, so he said to the miller, 'That's a talent that would please me hugely. If your daughter is as clever as you say, bring her to my palace tomorrow and I'll put her to the test.'

When the girl was brought to him, he led her to a room that was full of straw, gave her a spinning-wheel and said, 'Set to work. You have all night ahead of you. But if you haven't spun all this straw into gold by dawn, you must die.' Then he locked the door with his own hands and left her there alone.

The poor miller's daughter sat there without a clue what to do. She had no idea how to spin straw into gold and she grew more and more frightened and started to cry.

Suddenly the door opened and in came a little man who said, 'Good evening, Mistress Miller, why are you crying?'

'Oh, I have to spin this straw into gold and I don't know how to do it.'

'What will you give me if I do it for you?'

'My necklace.'

'Done.'

The little man took the necklace, squatted down before the spinning-wheel, and whirr, whirr, whirr! Three turns and the bobbin was full. And so he went on all night and at sunrise all the bobbins were full of gold.

First thing in the morning, in came the King and when he saw all the gold he was amazed and delighted. But the gold-greed grew in his heart and he had the miller's daughter taken to an even bigger room filled up with straw and told her to spin the lot into gold if she valued her life. She really didn't know what to do and was crying when the door opened. In stepped the little man again saying, 'What will you give me if I spin all this straw into gold?'

'The ring from my finger.'

So the little man took the ring and whirred away at the wheel all the long dark night and by dawn each dull strand of straw was glistening gold. The King was beside himself with pleasure at the treasure, but his desire for gold still wasn't satisfied. He took the miller's daughter to an even larger room full of straw and told her, 'You must spin all of this into gold tonight and if you succeed you shall be my wife.' And the King said to himself, 'She might only be the daughter of a miller, but I won't find a richer woman anywhere.'

As soon as the girl was alone, the little man appeared for the third time and said, 'What will you give me this time if I spin the straw into gold for you?'

'I have nothing left to give.'

'Then you must promise to give me the first child you have after you are Queen.'

'Who knows what the future holds,' thought the girl. And as she had no choice, she gave her word to the little man. At once he started to spin until all the straw was gold.

When the King arrived in the morning and saw everything just as he wished, he held the wedding at once and the miller's beautiful daughter became a Queen.

After a year she brought a gorgeous golden child into the world and thought no more of the little man. But one day he stepped suddenly into her room and said, 'Now give me what you promised.'

The Queen was truly horrified and offered him all the gold and riches of the kingdom if he would only leave the child. But the little man said, 'No. I'd rather have a living child than all the treasure in the world.' At this, the Queen began to sob so bitterly that the little man took pity on her and said, 'I'll give you three days. If you can find out my name by then, you can keep your child.'

The Queen sat up all night, searching her brains for his name like someone sieving for gold. She went through every single name she could think of. She sent out a messenger to ask everywhere in the land for all the names that could be found. On the next day, when the little man came, she recited the whole alphabet of names that she'd learned, starting with Balthasar, Casper, Melchior . . . But to each one the little man said, 'That isn't my name.'

On the second day, she sent servants all round the neighbourhood to find more names and she tried all the strange and unusual ones on the little man. 'Perhaps you're called Shortribs or Sheepshanks or Lacelegs.' But he always said, 'That isn't my name. On the third day, the messenger came back and said, 'I haven't managed to find a single new name, but as I approached a high mountain at the end of the forest, the place where fox and hare bid each other goodnight, I saw a small hut. There was a fire burning outside it and round the fire danced an absurd little man. He hopped on one leg and bawled:

> 'Bake today! Tomorrow brew!
> Then I'll take the young Queen's child!
> She will cry and wish she knew
> That RUMPELSTILTSKIN's how I'm styled!'

You may imagine how overjoyed the Queen was when she heard the name. And when soon afterwards the little man stalked in and demanded, 'Well, Mistress Queen, what is my name?', she started by saying, 'Is it Tom?' 'No.' 'Is it Dick?' 'No.' 'Is it Harry?' 'No.' 'Perhaps your name is Rumpelstiltskin?' 'The devil has told you! The devil has told you!' shrieked the little man. In his fury he stamped his right foot so hard on the ground that it went right in up to his waist. And then in a rage he pulled at his left leg so hard with the very same hands that had spun the straw into gold – that he tore himself in two.

Fair Katrinelje

'Good day, Father Hollowtree.' 'Thank you, Pif Paf Poltrie.' 'May I marry your daughter?' 'Oh, yes, if Mother Milkmoo, Brother Proudclogs, Sister Makecheese and the fair Katrinelje are willing you can marry her.'

'Then where is Mother Milkmoo?'
'She's in the barn a-milking the coo.'

'Good day, Mother Milkmoo.' 'Thank you, Pif Paf Poltrie.' 'May I marry your daughter?' 'Oh, yes, if Father Hollowtree, Brother Proudclogs, Sister Makecheese and the fair Katrinelje are willing, you can marry her.'

'Then where is Brother Proudclogs?'
'He's in the woodshed, a-chopping logs.'

'Good day, Brother Proudclogs.' 'Thank you, Pif Paf Poltrie.' 'May I marry your sister?' 'Oh, yes, if Father Hollowtree, Mother Milkmoo, Sister Makecheese and the fair Katrinelje are willing, you can marry her.'

'Then where is Sister Makecheese?'
'She's in the kitchen a-shelling peas.'

'Good day, Sister Makecheese.' 'Thank you, Pif Paf Poltrie.' 'May I marry your sister?' 'Oh, yes, if Father Hollowtree, Mother Milkmoo, Brother Proudclogs and the fair Katrinelje are willing, you can marry her.'

'Then where is the fair Katrinelje?'
'She's a-counting her pennies in the parlour.'

'Good day, fair Katrinelje.' 'Thank you, Pif Paf Poltrie.' 'Will you marry me?' 'Oh, yes, if Father Hollowtree,

Mother Milkmoo, Brother Proudclogs, Sister Makecheese are willing, then you can have me.'

'Fair Katrinelje, how much dowry do you have?'

'Fourteen pennies in hard cash, two-and-a-half pennies owing to me, half a pound of dried fruits, a quarter of roots and two ounces of shoots.

> 'All these things and more are mine.
> 'Don't you think my dowry's fine?'

'Pif Paf Poltrie, what is your trade? Are you a tailor?'

'Even better.'

'A cobbler?'

'Even better.'

'A ploughman?'

'Even better.'

'A joiner?'

'Even better.'

'A blacksmith?'

'Even better'

'A miller?'

'Even better.

'Perhaps you're a broom-maker.'

'Yes! So I am! And isn't that a splendid trade!'

Brother Scamp

Once there was a great war and when it was over many soldiers were discharged. One of these was Brother Scamp. He was given one loaf of ammunition-bread and four shillings and sent on his way. St Peter, however, had disguised himself as a beggarman and was sitting by the roadside. When Brother Scamp came along, he begged for charity. Brother Scamp answered him: 'Dear beggar man, what am I to give you? I have been a soldier, but on my dismissal I was given only this loaf of ammunition-bread and four shillings. Once they've gone, I shall have to beg myself. Even so, I'll give you something.' Then Brother Scamp divided his loaf into four parts, gave one to St Peter, and gave him a shilling as well.

The apostle thanked him and hurried on his way; but further along the road he sat down again disguised as a different beggar. When Brother Scamp came along, he begged for a gift as before. Brother Scamp spoke as he had earlier and again gave him a piece of bread and a shilling. St Peter thanked him and went on, but for the third time sat down in Brother Scamp's path disguised as a beggar. He begged again. Brother Scamp spoke as before and again gave him a quarter of bread and a shilling. St Peter thanked him.

Brother Scamp, with only one shilling and the last morsel of bread left, went on to an inn where he ate the bread and ordered a shilling's worth of ale. When he had finished, he set off once more and soon met St Peter, this time dressed-up as a discharged soldier like himself.

'Good day, comrade. Can you spare a bit of bread and a shilling for some beer?'

'Where would I find them?' said Brother Scamp. 'I've been discharged and all the army gave me was a loaf of ammunition-bread and four shillings. I met three beggars on the road and I gave each of them a quarter of bread and a shilling. I ate the last quarter of bread at an inn and spent the last shilling on ale. So now my pockets are empty. If you're in the same boat, then let us go begging together.'

St Peter said, 'There's no need to do that. I know a bit about healing. I'll soon earn as much as I need from that.'

'Well,' said Brother Scamp, 'I know nothing at all about that, so I'd better go begging on my own.'

'Just come along with me,' said St Peter, 'And if I make any money at it you can have half.'

'Fair enough,' said Brother Scamp, and the two soldiers went on their way together.

They soon came to a peasant's house, inside which they heard loud weeping and cries of lamentation. They went in. A man lay there, very sick and at death's door, and his poor wife was wailing her lungs out. 'Stop your weeping and wailing,' said St Peter, 'I will make this man well again.' He took some ointment from his pocket and healed the man quicker than an angel's wing. The man stood up in the best of health.

The husband and wife were overjoyed and said: 'How can we thank you? What can we give you to repay you?' But St Peter wouldn't accept any reward; and the more the peasant folk offered, the more he refused. Brother Scamp nudged St Peter: 'Take something, for God's sake. We need it!' Finally, the woman brought in a lamb and told St Peter that she really must take it. But St Peter didn't want to. Then Brother Scamp gave him a poke and said, 'Take it, take it. We need it.' At last St Peter said, 'All right, I'll accept it. But I won't carry it. If you want it so much, then you can carry it.' 'Fair enough,' said Brother Scamp, and hoisted the lamb onto his shoulder.

They journeyed on together and came to a forest. By now, Brother Scamp was beginning to find the lamb very heavy, and he was famished as well. So he said to his companion, 'Look, this is a good spot. Let's stop and cook the lamb and eat it.' 'If you like,' said St Peter, 'but I don't know anything about cooking. If you want to cook, there's a pot. I shall go for a walk until it's ready. But you mustn't start eating until I return. I will come back at the right time.' 'Off you go,' said Brother Scamp, 'I'm a nifty hand at cooking. Just leave everything to me.'

When St Peter had gone, Brother Scamp butchered the lamb, lit the fire, threw the meat into the pot and cooked it. After a while, the meat was ready, but St Peter still hadn't returned. Brother Scamp removed the meat from the pot, cut it up, and found the heart. 'That's supposed to be the best part,' he thought to himself. He tasted a little bit, then a little bit more, and a little bit more, and soon he had eaten it all up. Eventually, St Peter came back and said, 'You can eat the whole lamb yourself. Just give me the heart.'

Brother Scamp took a knife and fork and pretended to look for the heart. He poked and prodded anxiously among the flesh and finally gave up. 'There isn't any heart,' he said.

'How is that possible?' said St Peter.

'Search me,' said Brother Scamp. 'But hang on a minute! What fools we are! Everyone knows that a lamb hasn't got a heart.' 'Let's go then. If there's no heart, I don't want any lamb. You can have it all for yourself.'

'What I can't eat now, I'll take away in my knapsack,' said Brother Scamp. He ate up half the lamb and packed the rest into his knapsack.

They went on their way and after a while St Peter arranged for a great stream of water to block their path. They had to get across it and St Peter said, 'You go first.' But Brother Scamp said, 'No, you go first, comrade.' And he thought, 'If the water proves too deep for him, I can stay behind.'

St Peter waded across and the water only came up to his knees. So Brother Scamp followed him, but the water got deeper and deeper until it was up to his neck. Then he cried out, 'Brother! Help me!'

'Confess you ate the lamb's heart!'

'No! I didn't eat it!'

The water grew even deeper until it was up to his mouth. Brother Scamp cried out again, 'Brother! Help me!'

'Admit you ate the lamb's heart!'

'No! I didn't eat it!'

But St Peter would not have the man drown, so he made the water go down and helped him across.

They took to the road again and came to a kingdom where they heard that the King's daughter was ill and on the verge of death. The soldier turned to St Peter: 'Now then, Brother! This looks like just the thing for us. If we can cure her, we'll be set up for life!' St Peter agreed, but walked too slowly for Brother Scamp's liking. 'Come on, Brother, hurry up. We want to get there before it's too late.' But the more Brother Scamp pushed and prodded, the slower St Peter went; and before long they heard that the Princess had died.

'I knew it!' said Brother Scamp, 'This is what comes of your dawdling along.'

'Hold your tongue,' said St Peter, 'I don't just heal sick people. I can make dead people live again.'

'Well, if that's the case,' said Brother Scamp, 'Make sure we get a decent reward. Ask for half the kingdom at least.'

They went to the Royal Palace where everyone was distraught with grief. St Peter went straight to the King and vowed to him that he would bring his daughter back to life. He was taken to her room and said, 'Bring me a cauldron of water.'

They brought the water and he told everyone to leave the room except for Brother Scamp. St Peter cut off the dead girl's limbs and tossed them into the water. He made a fire under the cauldron and boiled them. When all the flesh had fallen off, he took the clean white bones out of the water, placed them on a table, and arranged them in the correct order. When he'd done all this to his satisfaction, he stepped forward and said three times, 'In the name of the Holy Trinity, dead Princess, stand up and live again.'

At the third time, the girl stood up, warm and healthy and beautiful. The King was shaking with joy and gratitude and said to St Peter, 'Name your reward. Even if you ask for half my kingdom you shall have it.' But St Peter replied, 'I want nothing.'

'Oh, you cabbage-head!' thought Brother Scamp. He nudged his comrade in the ribs and said, 'Don't be so stupid. You might not want a reward, but I do.' St Peter still wanted nothing, but the King saw that the other man felt quite the opposite and ordered his treasurer to fill Brother Scamp's knapsack with gold.

Again they went on their way. When they came to a forest, St Peter said to Brother Scamp, 'Now we'll share out the gold.' 'Fair enough.' St Peter divided the gold into three parts. Brother Scamp thought to himself, 'What nonsense has he got into his head now? Why divide the gold into three when there's only two of us?'

St Peter spoke: 'I've split the gold perfectly. One part for me, one for you, and one for whoever ate the lamb's heart.' 'That was me!' said Brother Scamp, and scooped up the gold as fast as a double-wink. 'I give you my word.'

'How is that possible,' said St Peter, 'When we know that a lamb has no heart?'

'What are you on about, Brother? Everyone knows a lamb has a heart just like any other animal. Why on earth shouldn't it?'

'Very well,' said St Peter, 'Keep the gold for yourself. I have had enough of your company and I'm going on by myself.'

'If that's what you want then fair enough, Brother,' the soldier said, 'Goodbye.'

So St Peter took a different road and Brother Scamp thought, 'I'm glad to see the back of him. What a strange individual he turned out to be.' He now had plenty of money, but he didn't know how to use it sensibly. He squandered some, gave some away, and after a while he was penniless once more. He came to a land where he was told that the King's daughter had died. He thought to himself, 'Hang about! There might be something in this for me. I'll bring her back to life and make sure I get a decent reward.' So he went straight to the King and offered to return his daughter from the dead. The King had heard that there was a discharged soldier going around bringing the dead back to life. He thought that Brother Scamp might be this man, but he wasn't certain. So he asked the advice of his counsellor, who said that, since his daughter was dead, he had nothing to lose.

Brother Scamp requested a cauldron of water and ordered everyone from the room. Then he severed the dead girl's limbs, tossed them into the water, lit a fire, exactly as he had seen St Peter do. The water bubbled up. When the flesh fell away from the bones, he took them out and lay them on the table; but he had no idea of the correct order and got the beautiful white bones all jumbled up. Nevertheless, he stepped up to the table and cried, 'In the name of the Holy Trinity, rise from the dead.' He said it three times but not a bone budged. He said it three times more, but it was useless, and he shouted 'Blasted girl! Get up off that table or I'll half-kill you!'

The words had no sooner left his mouth when St Peter came in through the window, once again disguised as a discharged soldier.

'Blasphemous godless man!' he said, 'What are you doing? How can the poor girl rise again when you've got her bones in such a mess!' 'I've done the best I could, Brother,' said Brother Scamp. 'I'll help you out just this once,' said St Peter, 'but if you ever try anything like this again, Heaven help you. Furthermore, you are neither to demand nor accept any reward at all from the King.'

Then St Peter arranged the bones in the right order and said three times, 'In the name of the Holy Trinity rise from the dead.' The King's daughter breathed and arose, as healthy and beautiful as she always was, and St Peter went out through the window. Brother Scamp was pleased things had worked out so well, but annoyed at not being allowed to ask for his reward.

'That bloke's not the full shilling,' he thought, 'What he gives with one hand he takes away with the other. It's beyond me!'

The King offered Brother Scamp any reward he wanted. He refused, as he'd been ordered to, but with hints, winks, nudges, shuffles and shrugs, he got the King to fill his knapsack with gold and off he went.

St Peter was waiting at the Palace gate. 'Just look at you! Didn't I forbid you to accept anything? And yet out you march as bold as brass with your knapsack bulging with gold.'

'I can't help it if they forced it on me,' said Brother Scamp.

'You'd better not try this sort of thing again or you'll wish you hadn't.'

'Have no fear on that score, Brother. Why should I bother to boil bones when I'm loaded with gold?'

'I can imagine how long your gold will last you,' said St Peter. 'But to keep you from meddling in forbidden ways again, I'll grant you the power to wish anything you please into your knapsack. Now goodbye to you. You will not see me again.'

'Goodbye,' said Brother Scamp and thought, "Good riddance more like, you peculiar person. I shan't be running to catch up with you!' And he gave no more thought to the magical power of his knapsack.

Brother Scamp travelled on with his gold, and squandered and wasted it the same as before. When he only had four shillings left, he came to an inn. 'I might as well spend them,' he thought, and ordered up three shillings worth of wine and one of bread. He sat drinking and the smell of roast goose filled his nostrils. When he looked around he saw two geese that the inn-keeper was cooking in the oven. Suddenly he remembered that his companion had told him he could wish anything he pleased into his knapsack. 'Oh ho!' he thought, 'Let's see if it works with the geese.' He went outside and said, 'I wish those two geese were out of the oven and in my knapsack!' After saying the words, he unbuckled the knapsack, looked in, and there they were. 'This couldn't be better!' he said 'I'm a made man!'

He sat down in a meadow and took out the geese. As he was busily eating, two journeymen came along and looked hungrily at the goose that hadn't been touched yet. Brother Scamp thought to himself 'One goose is plenty for me,' and called over the two journeymen. 'Here, take this goose and wish me well as you eat it.' They thanked him, went into the inn, ordered a flask of wine and a loaf of bread, took out Brother Scamp's goose and began to eat. The inn-keeper's wife had been watching them and said to her husband, 'That pair over there are eating a goose. Go and check it's not one of ours out of the oven.'

He went and looked and the oven was worse than gooseless. 'Hoy, you thieves! You think you're getting that goose pretty cheap, don't you? Pay up at once or I'll stripe your skins with a stick.' 'We're not thieves,' they protested, 'A discharged soldier gave us the goose out there in the meadow.'

'Don't try and pull the wool over my eyes,' said the inn-keeper, 'There was a soldier here but he went out the door empty-handed. I saw him myself. You're the thieves and you'd better pay up.' But they couldn't pay, so he seized his stick and swiped them out of the inn.

Brother Scamp continued on his way and came to a place where there was a magnificent castle, and not far from it a wretched inn. He went to the inn and asked for a bed for the night, but the inn-keeper refused him, saying 'There is no room. The house is full of noblemen.' Brother Scamp said, 'That's odd. Why would they choose this place instead of that splendid castle?' 'Well, you see,' said the inn-keeper, 'it's not easy to spend a night in that castle. Some have tried, but no one has ever come out alive.'

'If others have tried, so will I,' said Brother Scamp.

'Don't even think of it,' said mine host. 'It will be the end of you.'

But Brother Scamp insisted: 'Don't worry about me. Just give me the keys and something to eat and drink.'

So the man gave him the keys and some food and wine and Brother Scamp went into the castle and enjoyed his meal. After a while, he felt sleepy and lay down on the floor because there was no bed. He soon fell fast asleep, but in the middle of the night was awakened by a terrifying noise. When he opened his eyes, he saw nine ugly devils dancing round him in a circle. 'Dance as much as you like,' said Brother Scamp, 'But stay away from me.' The devils came closer and closer and nearly stepped on his face with their hideous feet.

'Stop it, you fiends!' he cried, but their frenzy got worse. Brother Scamp became very angry and shouted, 'Quiet, I said!' He grabbed a table-leg and set about them with it, but nine devils were too many for one soldier. While he was hitting the one in front of him, the ones behind him grabbed his hair and yanked fiercely. 'Stinking devils! This is too much. But now I'll show you something. All nine of you into my knapsack!' Wheesh! In they all went. He buckled the knapsack, flung it into a corner, and at last everything was still. Brother Scamp lay down again and slept until morning. The inn-keeper and the nobleman who owned the castle arrived to see what had happened to him. They were astonished to find him alive and well and asked, 'Didn't the ghosts harm you?'

'How could they harm me? I've got them all in my knapsack. Now you can live in your castle again. The ghosts won't bother you any more.'

The nobleman thanked him, rewarded him generously and begged him to stay in his service and he would provide for him till death. But Brother Scamp said, 'No, I'm used to wandering about. I'll just get on my way.'

Back on the road, Brother Scamp stopped at a smithy, put the knapsack full of devils on the anvil, and asked the blacksmith and his apprentices to batter it with all their might. The devils screamed dreadfully, and when he opened the knapsack eight were dead, but one, who had been in a crease, was still alive. That one scuttled away and went to Hell.

After this, Brother Scamp travelled about for a long time, and if anyone knows what he got up to, they'll have a long tale to tell. Finally, he grew old and his thoughts turned to death; so he went to a hermit who was respected as a Holy Man and said: 'I'm tired of knocking about, and now I want to see about getting in to the Kingdom of Heaven.' The hermit replied, 'There are two roads. One is broad and pleasant and leads to Hell. The other is narrow and rough and leads to Heaven.' Brother Scamp thought, 'I'd be daft to take the rough and narrow way.' Sure enough, he took the broad, pleasant way and fetched up at a big black gate.

It was the Gate of Hell. He knocked, and the gate-keeper squinted out to see who was there. When he saw Brother Scamp, he nearly leapt out of his skin, for he just happened to be the ninth devil in the knapsack who'd escaped with only a black eye. Fast as a rat, he slammed, locked and bolted the gate, and fled to the Head Devil.

'There's a man outside with a knapsack,' he said. 'He wants to come in, but for Hell's sake don't let him, or he'll wish all Hell into his knapsack. He had me in it once, and what a terrible pounding I got!'

Brother Scamp was told he couldn't come in and should clear off. 'If they won't give me a welcome here,' he thought, 'I'll see if there's room for me in Heaven. I've got to stay somewhere.'

So he turned around and travelled until he came to the Gate of Heaven, and knocked upon it. St Peter happened to be on duty as gate-keeper, and Brother Scamp recognised him right away. 'Well, look who it is!' he thought. 'My old comrade will give me a warmer reception.'

But St Peter said, 'I don't believe it! You think you can get into Heaven?'

'Let me in, Brother, I've got to go somewhere. They wouldn't take me in Hell, or I wouldn't be standing here now.'

'Too bad,' said Peter, 'You're not getting in here.'

'Well,' said Brother Scamp, 'If you really won't allow me in then take back your knapsack, because I don't want to keep anything of yours.'

'Hand it over then,' said St Peter.

He passed the knapsack through the railings and St Peter hung it up behind his chair.

'Now,' said Brother Scamp, 'I wish myself into the knapsack.'

Whoosh! There he was in the knapsack, the knapsack was in Heaven, and St Peter had to let him stay there, fair enough.